MVFOL

BARNACLE LOVE

BARNACLE

Anthony De Sa

LOVE

ALGONQUIN BOOKS OF CHAPEL HILL   2010

Published by

Algonquin Books of Chapel Hill

Post Office Box 2225

Chapel Hill, North Carolina 27515-2225

a division of

Workman Publishing

225 Varick Street

New York, New York 10014

First published in Canada by Anchor Canada, 2008.

Design by Terri Nimmo.

Grateful acknowledgment is made to the following for
permission to reprint previously published material:

"Caged Bird," copyright © 1983 by Maya Angelou, from *Shaker, Why Don't
You Sing?* by Maya Angelou. Used by permission of Random House, Inc.

Excerpt from the essay "Nothing Personal" from *The Price of the Ticket:
Collected Non-Fiction 1945–1985*, by James Baldwin. Published by
St. Martin's Press, New York. Reprinted by arrangement with
The James Baldwin Estate.

This is a work of fiction. While, as in all fiction, the literary
perceptions and insights are based on experience, all names,
characters, places, and incidents either are products of the
author's imagination or are used fictitiously.

Library of Congress Cataloging-in-Publication
De Sa, Anthony.
Barnacle love / Anthony De Sa.—1st pbk. ed.
    p. cm.
ISBN 978-1-56512-926-9
1. Portuguese—Canada—Fiction.   2. Domestic fiction.   I. Title.
PR9199.4.D486B37 2010
813'.6—dc22   2010020929

10 9 8 7 6 5 4 3 2 1
First Paperback Edition

In memory of my mother and father

Contents

Part I   Terra Nova

Of God and Cod   3
Reason to Blame   29
Fado   51
Made of Me   71
Barnacle Love   97

Part II   Caged Birds Sing

Urban Angel   119
Shoeshine Boy   143
Senhor Canada   161
Pounding Their Shadows   177
Mr. Wong Presents Jesus   195

Acknowledgments   215

BARNACLE LOVE

~ I ~

TERRA NOVA

For nothing is fixed, forever and forever and forever, it is not fixed; the earth is always shifting, the light is always changing, the sea does not cease to grind down rock. Generations do not cease to be born, and we are responsible to them because we are the only witnesses they have. The sea rises, the light fails, lovers cling to each other, and children cling to us. The moment we cease to hold each other, the sea engulfs us and the light goes out.

James Baldwin

~ OF GOD AND COD ~

THERE IS NOTHING HE CAN DO. He is lifted high into the air by the swells that roll, break, and crash upon themselves. His dory is smashed, the flotsam scattered: pieces of white jagged wood afloat, tangled in knotted rope, nothing much to grab hold of before the ocean lifts him higher, only to drop him into its turbulent waters, catching him in the current. Again, he pierces the surface, the biting cold filling his lungs as he coughs and sputters. It is the moment he needs. He reaches into his sweater and draws out the crucifix, which glistens in the moon's light. He twirls it between puckered fingers, places it in his mouth—between his clicking teeth. He feels its weight and shape cushioned on his tongue, closes his blue lips and allows himself to let go, to sink beneath the foaming surface into the dark molasses sea.

Big Lips. Are you here?

~

The Portuguese call it *saudade:* a longing for something so indefinite as to be indefinable. Love affairs, miseries of life, the way things were, people already dead, those who left and the ocean that tossed them on the shores of a different land—all things born of the soul that can only be felt.

Manuel Antonio Rebelo was a product of this passion. He grew up with the tales of his father, a man who held two things most sacred, God and cod—*bacalhau*—and not always in that order. His father's words formed vivid pictures of grizzled brave fishermen and whale hunters who left their families for months to fish the great waters off Terra Nova, the new land. Visions of mothers shrouded in black, of confused wives—the pregnant ones feeling alone, the others glad for the respite from pregnancy—spun in his mind. And then there were the scoured children, waving in their Sunday finery. The small boys bound in worn but neatly pressed blazers and creased shorts. The little girls scattered like popcorn in their outgrown Communion dresses as they watched their fathers' ascents onto magnificent ships. In his dreams Manuel saw the men with their torn and calloused hands, faces worn, dark and toughened by the salted mist. As a child he would sit by the cliffs for hours, dangling his bare feet over the side of the hundred-foot drop to the shore, kicking the rock with his pink heels, placing his hands over his eyes to shield the sunlight, already yearning for the fading figures of the White Fleet.

"One day I'll disappear," he'd say aloud.

He could make out the faint shadow of a large fish that circled just under the skinned surface of the water.

"Did you hear that, Big Lips?" he shouted.

As if in response, the large grouper seemed to stop. Manuel could see the fish's fins fanning against the mottled blue and green of the ocean's rocky shallows. He had once befriended one of these gentle giants. The villagers believed that these fish could live for up to one hundred years. This was in part due to the story of Eduarda Ramos, one of the village midwives, who insisted she had reclaimed her wedding band from the belly of a large grouper her son had caught—fifty-three years after she had lost the ring while cleaning some fish by the shore.

As the large fish swam away and disappeared into the ocean's darker depths, Manuel couldn't help but wonder if the fish he had named was still alive. If the fish he had just seen was Big Lips.

Manuel's yearning became a palpable ache. The Azores held nothing for him. The tiny island of São Miguel was suffocating, lost as it was in the middle of the Atlantic. Early in life he knew the world his mother had formed for him was too small, too predictable. He was the oldest boy. But it wasn't for this reason alone that Manuel carried the burden of his mother's dreams. He bore a close resemblance to his father: the liquid steel color of his eyes, his thick stubborn mound of blond hair, and the round angelic features of his face. The blunt noses, darker skin, and almost black, shrimp-like eyes that adorned his siblings had been borrowed from his mother's side. Manuel thought they were all pretty and he loved them, but he also knew that in his mother's mind they held no promise.

"You are your father's son. He lives in you," she'd sigh. "You possess his greatness." Manuel felt her breasts pressed flat against his back, her sharp chin digging into his head. "I can smell it in your breath's sweetness."

Maria had plucked Manuel out of her brood and he became the chosen one. Her ambitions for her son were firm rather than clear: Manuel would become a man of importance, learned and respected in the village and beyond. He would have the advantage of private tutors, which meant his siblings would need to keep the bottoms of their shoes stuffed with corn husks to clog the holes and keep their feet dry. Manuel was often ashamed of himself as he walked up Rua Nova with his brothers and sisters, his polished shoes shining like the blue-black of a mussel. He would be taught a rigorous catechism by the village priest, Padre Carlos. The teachings of God would make him fair and virtuous.

"It's all for you, *filho*," she'd say, often in front of her other children as they went about, cowering, in their daily chores. It was only because they loved Manuel and never once blamed him for anything they were denied that he began to resent his mother's cruelty.

His ten-year-old brother Jose came home one day with a sick calf that he walked through the front door and into their narrow dark hallway. Everyone smiled and watched as the brother who loved animals above anything else tugged at the sickly calf, urged it out the back door toward a patch of tall grass. But the pastoral calm was interrupted by the sharp crack of dry wood. Manuel saw his young brother fall to the packed-earth floor like a ball of dough. His cheek lay pressed against the floor, he was afraid to lift his head. He licked the blood that trickled from the corner of his mouth. Manuel looked to his mother, who held the splintered end of the broom over her shoulder. She picked the boy up by the scruff of his collar and he dangled from her clenched fist.

"You get this filthy beast out of here. This is our home, not a barn," her voice shook.

Jose turned the nervous animal around and, still in a daze, directed the reluctant calf back out the front door. Albina and the others continued their work. Maria Theresa da Conceição Rebelo sat back down on the chair and poured the beans into the sagging lap of her apron. Manuel picked up the broom. Looking straight at his mother, he flung the broken handle across the kitchen. The stoneware bowls that had been carefully set on the barnboard table smashed. He heard the drawn breaths of his sisters. His mother stood and the beans sprung from her apron across the floor. She cocked her hand over her shoulder. He stood still for what seemed like an eternity, challenging her with his glare. She lowered her arm as he stormed after his brother.

He was twelve then. Manuel vowed that somehow he would make it all better. Freedom would provide opportunities for his siblings. But first, he would have to save himself.

Now, at the age of twenty, Manuel maintained an indifference to Maria's ambitions. Every spring he would venture to the same spot and perch himself on the overhang. He would look out to the sea, feel the warming winds against his pale smooth skin. His still-boyish cowlick pressed against his forehead. He'd carefully roll each of his socks into a ball, stuff them into his new leather shoes, to kick his now yellowed heels against the cliff wall with a vigor that had only intensified during the months he had spent in the mildewed Banco Micaelense, counting out *escudos* with a vacant smile, throwing open all windows to breathe in the sea, hearing Amalia's despair on the radio, her riveting outbursts of emotion. He knew it was time to tell his mother.

"*Mãe*, I'm going away for a while," he said.

She continued to hang the laundry on the line, the stubborn stains facing the house, the cleaner sides billowing toward the neighbours. She held wooden clothespins in her mouth—sometimes three at a time—securely between her crowded teeth.

"*Mãe*, look at me," he urged. "I need to go. I need to be part of a bigger world. I need to know if there's room out there for me."

Her job was only interrupted for a fraction of a second. Manuel realized she had been waiting for this. Only yesterday she had walked into the bank, and he had noticed a disguised sadness in her step as she approached him in his white shirt and tie; she had pressed the shirt that morning and was pleased that the crease in his cuff had held. She continued hanging the clothes as if she hadn't heard. But Manuel could sense her anger, the disappointment in allowing herself to believe it was possible for her children to want for themselves the same things she did. Maria Theresa da Conceição Rebelo stopped. Manuel looked away for a moment to catch the silhouettes of his brothers and sisters behind the muslin curtains of the house. Albina was twenty-two and the oldest child. Her hands rested on their young brothers, Mariano and Jose. They were eighteen, only ten months apart. Candida was fifteen and sat on the sill with her back leaning against the drapes. He had expected them to be there, listening from inside their shared bedrooms. He chose to move his blurred vision back toward his mother. His eyes traveled up to her hair, to the wisps that looped up, barely held by her hair comb. *When did her hair turn gray?* he thought.

"*Mãe—*"

"You look like your father."

She walked toward the house wiping her hands on a torn apron, kicking with her bare feet the feeding hens that got in her way. As she reached the door, she bent down and scooped one of the hens up and under her freckled arm. Turning to face her son, she stroked the chicken's head with her free hand before her swollen, red fingers closed around its thin neck and tugged, just one quick yank before the bird's head fell, still jerking.

"Your supper will be ready soon," and she slammed the door.

They had not spoken. The night before he left, his mother had locked herself in her room. He found a package, brown folded paper tied neatly with trussing string, outside her bedroom door. He knew she wouldn't come out. It had been too painful the first time, fifteen years back, when she had wrapped some cheese, bread, *chouriço,* and a few loose sheets of paper and bundled them all together with an embroidered dishtowel before she embraced her husband Antonio for the last time.

Manuel untied the knots, their whorls flicking against the parcel. He stood in front of her door, hoping she'd hear the rustling of paper. He was mindful of refolding the paper and rolling the string into a ball his mother could use it again. In the parcel, Manuel found a yellowed fisherman's sweater smelling of ocean and, in a tiny envelope made of tin wrap, his father's gold crucifix and chain. They were the only things that she had left of her husband; his body had been buried at sea. There were no words written on the paper or in the folds. He checked. He tried knocking, then stopped after three soft raps and put his lips to the door, touching the grain.

"*Adeus, Mãe,*" he whispered.

He couldn't recall exactly what his father looked like, only his blue-gray eyes and warm smile. But he did remember sitting on his father's knee and looking for the gleaming crucifix buried in his father's chest hair. This was the same chain that he now placed around his neck. He swung the sweater under his arm and tossed his duffel bag over his shoulder, his fingers whitened by the strain. Later, tucked in his socks or wrapped in his underwear, Manuel would discover the gifts secretly offered, for fear of their mother's disapproval, by his siblings: Albina's embroidered *M* handkerchief, the copper whistle Jose used to herd cattle, and Mariano's pocket knife. Also in his bag, pressed between his cotton undershirts, was a black-and-white photograph of

Candida, lips pursed like a Hollywood actress caught in a hazy cloud of smoke. Manuel walked down the silent corridor and out the front door.

He arrived in the cobbled square of Ponte Delgada before daybreak. The rigged ships waited, tethered to the docks; their white sails reflected the morning moon but barely rippled in the early breeze behind the makeshift altar. The altar had been constructed on the docks and bore the symbol of an intertwined cross and anchor. The sails would form the backdrop for the traditional farewell mass. Soon the square would be filled with crowds pushing their way up to the front, wanting to be touched by the priest, blessed by his hand.

Manuel once understood that desire and need. He had reached out as a young boy when faced with the loss of his father. But his trust had been betrayed and his want silenced. He hadn't thought of Padre Carlos for a while. Some things were best pushed far back into the dark places of the mind. But the impending voyage, his mother's inability to understand his decision, had awakened the loneliness he had felt as a boy.

"Those who serve me, serve God," Padre Carlos had whispered.

He could still feel the priest's hot breath behind his ear.

"It's between us and God. Do you understand?"

He shook his head, trying to drive away the fear and anger he still held for the priest his mother had entrusted with her young son.

He opened his eyes to the early sky, ribbons of gold and pink, and the sounds of families trickling in to claim the coveted spots closest to the altar. The altar boys were busy preparing for mass, and the pesky vendors with their bloated and teetering carts encircled the square, droning, *"Pequeno almoço! . . . Pão torrado, queijo! . . . Pequeno almoço!"* Manuel responded to the stabs of the man's nasal voice announcing breakfast by fumbling in his pocket for some *escudos.*

"And as these brave men leave for the cold and foggy seas, we pray for them—for their work and sacrifice." The priest paused for effect, then the homily continued toward its crescendo.

"And we stay behind: mothers, wives, children. We remain! . . . And with us remains the promise that only God can return them safely to us." He lowered his head.

Manuel looked around. *Maybe they came,* he allowed himself to hope. He stopped himself by swinging his duffel hard over his back.

He would be one of fifty-three men on board. Together, they would spend days thrown against the ship's hull, stomachs churning with only the veined whites of their eyes exposed to the bitter spring cold. He was the first to walk past the embracing clusters, the wailing women and the oblivious children. He boarded the *Argus,* made his way down into her belly to begin the 1954 *campanha.* Unlike the other men on board who ventured and risked their lives for God, country, and family, Manuel knew that he would risk his life for a new beginning. He didn't look back.

~

The pounding of the sea was relentless. During the long days, the men talked of the foreign trawlers that hauled in thousands of pounds of cod while no man's life was endangered.

"But we are Portuguese . . . we need to protect the traditions of the fisherman." Manuel heard these words. His eyes caught the streaks of orange embers coming from their cigarettes, their bodies dark and unseen as their hands gesticulated in circles or slashes only to stop and glow with every inhalation. "One man, one boat, one line dropped to the depths of the ocean," another man in the huddle finished the sentiment. Manuel had remained silent for days. When he wasn't retching into a tin pail from the constant motion or covering his nose and mouth with his sweater to filter the dank odors that wafted beneath the deck, he listened and learned: heard the men call him *Boneco*—doll, because of his big blue eyes and round face.

Once off the Grand Banks, each man was assigned his own wooden dory that dangled precariously off the side of the mother ship. These fourteen-foot vessels would be their homes through the long days of fishing. The thrashing cod were the only guests invited on board. At four o'clock in the morning the men were lowered into the black ocean, to push off immediately from the vessel—once one hit water, a wave could be fatal, crashing the dory into the side of the *Argus,* destroying the craft and killing the man. For some of these old dorymen it was their fortieth voyage. Francisco Battista Rego was the oldest. Inscrutable, at sixty-two he had visited the Grand Banks forty-three times, so often in fact he said that he had forgotten what a summer in his native Terceira was like. The seas called out to him, and for months he left his wife and children. For six months of the year—from May to October—these men were his family, a family he had come to know more intimately than his own.

One night, as the men slept up against each other so as to keep warm, Francisco *Golfinho,* the dolphin, snuggled up to Manuel *Boneco.*

"I'll watch over you," Golfinho whispered.

He reached over and grabbed Manuel's hand, pulled him closer.

"Don't panic, show no fear—the panicked are dead."

Manuel could see the man's stubby fingers, made rounder by his missing fingernails, encase his own smallish hand—as a father's would his son's. He thought of his own father and was comforted by Francisco's protective words that came when Manuel felt loneliest, most vulnerable. Other men had busied themselves with writing letters to wives, mothers, children, or brothers— someone back home who needed to know they were alive and well. He could not write home, not with the way things had been left. Only shattered images remained. But the act of writing soothed him, so Manuel began to write letters also. They all began with "Dear Big Lips . . ." Then, in the cool pink of daybreak, he'd move up on deck and let shredded pieces of paper slip from his fingers like confetti.

He was physically drained. Here they all were, hand-lining for cod from their dory boats all day, only to return to the ship at sundown to begin splitting, gutting, and salting the day's catch. It was the brandy, the songs, and the old yarns repeated by tired, dizzy men that kept them alive. And every morning they would once again prepare to descend into the sea, push off from the *Argus* and venture far through the thick fog to drop their lines two or three hundred feet into the abyss.

Manuel awaited the promise that the tedious months in their berths would be broken occasionally by a visit to St. John's, when the ship would make a scheduled call to replenish supplies, make repairs to sails or engines, and provide shore leave. Other times there was a need to land injured men or just to seek some shelter from the storms that tore across the sheet of black water and tossed the White Fleet like toy boats. He had heard of how the fishermen became a prominent part of Newfoundland life. They visited the Fishermen's Centre and window-shopped along Water and Duckworth streets with the bits of money they had to spend. They remembered their families back home, buying souvenirs: toys, stockings, perfume, toothpaste. At the post office, the men sent mail home or picked up parcels they had ordered the year before from the Eaton's catalogue.

One Saturday morning, word spread along the crowded bunks that the fleet would finally call into St. John's before returning home. Manuel could scarcely contain his excitement. A blend of joy and confusion tumbled among the men. Some howled with pleasure as they mockingly groped each other like passionate lovers, or practiced their English out loud: broken words and phrases like *how much?* or *you look beautiful today.* Many went looking for comforts, a clean girl, and certain houses were glad to provide them.

Manuel had dressed carefully and made his way to the deck. He held on to the smooth railing, leaned his torso over the open sea as if to breathe in churning air. Some of the men ran naked on the upper deck, drew up cold sea water and doused themselves, rubbed their goose-pimpled limbs and their stubbled necks with amber bars of glycerin soap. Manuel closed his eyes and then opened them again to catch the rhythmic beacon atop the outline of a distant shore. It was *Cabo de Espera,* the "cape of waiting," as the Portuguese had named it. He had waited so long and it was only now that it had become so palpable. Manuel smiled.

Many of the veteran fishermen seemed amused by the frenetic energy that consumed the younger men. Manuel couldn't help but think they were recalling a time when they would have been swept into the madness. Now, they appeared content to save their money and make a bit more by sitting on the piers, mending sails or repairing the long lines of hooks as they smoked and drank Portuguese wine. Many of the residents bought things from the fishermen, indulgences like cigarettes and wine. Some men had even developed relationships with families in St. John's.

Before coming up on deck Manuel had allowed himself to feel a moment of guilt for abandoning his mother's dream. He had carefully made his bed, the way he had been taught. He was afraid, and yet he knew it was the only way in which he could construct a future, for him and for them.

The *Argus*'s hull kissed the pier's concrete side. Manuel scanned the enormous wharves, looked up toward the city of St. John's as the ship's horn blew and a group of pigeons lighted and flew across his view like a net cast against the open sea.

He stepped onto the gangway and slowly descended. The morning sun bathed the regular facades of the port buildings, with their pitched roofs and masonry walls, that stood along the road. With every step his eyes caught the white or yellow gabled trim, the paved roads and flash of glass. Angular shadows that splayed across sidewalks. He looked up to the teetering city built in tiers, splattered with green, vermilion, and white clapboard houses. It was so different from the whitewashed world he came from, and the moment his feet touched solid ground he knew that this place was his promised land.

It wasn't difficult to find his way around. Manuel simply followed the throngs of fishermen as he dodged the cars and trucks that sputtered past on both sides of the narrow road. His first stop was at the Arcade store, where a pile of white shoes greeted him. He was told that the locals called these Portuguese sneakers, something even the poorest of fishermen could afford. Manuel was stunned by the sheer amounts of clothing and food; shelves stocked all the way to the edge, some things piled two or three high. The weight on these shelves made their centers sag close to the worn wooden floors. He didn't know where to begin.

"Can I help you?"

Manuel turned to meet an attractive woman with a slight overbite that made her upper lip look full when her mouth was closed. She was slightly older than Manuel, twenty-five or so, he thought. She did not look at him, simply looked down, held her thin fingers clasped in front of her, and swung her body from side to side.

"Thank you," Manuel managed to say.

He crouched to look up into her eyes. His inquisitive gesture made her smile. Her eyebrows were thin and penciled. Her mossy green eyes were set wide apart, made wider by the way her hair was pulled into a ponytail.

"Is that the size you want?" she asked, pointing at the shoes he held tucked under his arm.

"*Irmão. Irmão.*"

"Mary!" she called out. She then lowered her voice when she saw him twitch. "Mary, he's talkin' in Portuguese. Don't know what I'm saying," she added.

"Brother. For my brother," came out of his mouth, as if in answer.

"That's better," she said. "Now what size is your brother? What size, though?"

He looked down at her gold name tag: *Linda.* He pointed to her name and mouthed the word in a nervous stutter. When she smiled he continued, "Is mean beautiful in Portuguese." Her face flushed red and her head tilted to the side.

"Anything else I can help you with?"

Linda had wrapped the gifts he had purchased in their own separate packets: shoes for his brothers and slips and stockings for his sisters—he smiled to himself remembering the embarrassing gestures made to Linda in his attempt to describe what he wanted. For his mother he had found a tortoiseshell hair comb, encrusted with small crystals along its scalloped edge. He knew that she would think it was too dear for her to wear, but he wanted her to have something nice. Manuel had insisted that Linda clearly write the names of his siblings on their respective packets. He couldn't help but notice her relief when he used the word *sister* as she scrawled Albina and Candida on the stiff brown parchment. Everything needed to be wrapped well, for the packets would be sent home by mail. Linda directed him to the post office.

Once relieved of his parcels, Manuel was guided by a couple of other Portuguese fishermen to where Mateus lived, a man known to provide the comforts of home to seafaring men. He did not enter the home located just below the towering gloom of the Basilica of St. John the Baptist. He had been avoiding the church ever since he landed. Manuel simply stood outside Mateus's house and bathed in the familiar sounds of the accordion and trill voices of amateur *fadistas.* He knew that here he would find wine and food but most importantly, he knew inside was the man who had lived in St. John's since he was a boy. The man had left Portugal hidden in the dory of the ship, in search of his father. The man would help Manuel.

Manuel spent the rest of his day weaving in and out of shops, dizzied by the display of things to buy: coffee, sugar, and vegetables he had never seen. He saw women smoking casually as they moved along the hills that undulated upward to the church. There were men in suits and hats who walked along with purpose and importance. They angled their shoulders so as not to hit the narrow bay windows that jutted every so often into the crowded sidewalks. Other men lumbered along the roads in coveralls or thigh-high rubber boots, pushing carts or lugging crates over their shoulders. Manuel saw a Chinese man sorting through vegetables and felt compelled to follow him up a narrow series of steps, past a war statue, up to yet another layer of the city to be explored. Manuel looked up at a large sign with a panda bear sipping from a bowl. He opened the door and heard the tinkling of chimes. Manuel twirled the noodles on his fork—he wasn't quite sure what the sticks that lay next to his plate were for—and forced the swirling mounds of sweetly covered noodles and scored lengths of squid into his mouth.

After his meal he continued to walk through the streets of the city. He didn't worry about getting lost. From almost any point in St. John's he could look out toward the Narrows and into the sea. He could then let his eyes work their way back to the wharf, where he could see the White Fleet's forest of masts and sails. He could see the long lengths of rope and chain that held the ships firmly against the dock. Some ropes had been covered in long underwear and plaid flannel shirts that flapped in the warm air. He could see the decks of the ships covered with the dory sails, allowed to dry in the waning summer sun.

Tired, Manuel found a spot in a park at the top of the hill. He sat under the shade of a tree, surrounded by the magnificent homes where all the rich, fine men lived, he assumed.

Manuel recognized a few of the Portuguese fishermen playing soccer in their bare feet. Some young boys played with them. Soon there were people gathering to sit on benches or sprawl on checked blankets. They watched the game played in the meadow near the bandstand as the dark-skinned Portuguese players dazzled everyone with their footwork. The grunting only drew louder claps at the friendly sportsmanship. Manuel took off his shoes and socks in the comfort of sounds and sights familiar but new. He flicked the cool blades of grass between his toes. A sailor began playing his accordion—some lilting Portuguese waltzes—under the roof of the bandstand. With the music dancing in his head, Manuel turned and looked out to the sparkling, still water in the harbor. *Life in this new land is determined by being so close to the ocean,* he thought. It was as if the cliff he had dangled his feet from all his life was the same rock and mineral that formed along the shores of this land. The drift may have occurred millions of years before but there was sameness, an intimate sense of belonging that closed the chasm of ocean between here and his home—between all things left behind and his future.

Manuel's eyes had grown heavy and he had fallen asleep. His eyes opened slightly at the sound of the first gust of foghorns blowing. Manuel drew his knees close to his chest and wrapped his arms around his legs. The park now lay empty in front of him. He could see sails crawling up the masts and the men filing in thin lines like ants, winding their way down the streets toward the docks.

The time spent on land had been short. The men boarded the ship wearily, their minds drunk with stories just waiting to be told. There were only a few days left before the *Argus* and other ships would turn their noses home, and underneath the layer of fatigue were the fired spirits of men who knew they would be with their real families soon. But the promise of the new land would not be erased from Manuel's mind. He closed his eyes in the warm knowledge he would stay.

The foghorns blared again.

The wind had picked up in the dusk and Manuel reached for his father's sweater, which he had knotted around his waist. He pulled it over his head. With a desperate hope, he thrust his hand up under his sweater and patted his chest. His mind's veil lifted and he pictured his father's gold crucifix in its foil packet pressed under the center of his mattress. There was no hesitation as he clambered down the steep hills toward the wharf. There were times when he thought he would stumble down the sloping streets, that his burning thighs wouldn't be able to stop the momentum building with every leap. He sprung onto the ramp, pushed himself through the thick clumps of returning men. Manuel's boots clanged against the iron mesh gangway, the metallic sound reverberating in his panicked head. He reached the mouth of the doorway, threw himself down its gullet in a single bound, felt the walls like a blind man, pupils ill-adjusted to the gloom as he charged into an open room strewn with narrow rows of rotting bunks. He flipped over his mattress and grabbed at the tinfoil envelope. He unfolded the flaps and drew out the twirling cross.

The foghorns blew again, deep and long.

Manuel leapt up the stairs in a fluid motion, the necklace now secured beneath his father's sweater. As he came up on deck, Manuel's eyes met Francisco Golfinho's clean-shaven face and tender stare. Manuel looked over

Francisco's shoulder to the city of St. John's. He pushed up against Francisco, tried to wedge himself between some men who sang in a drunken stupor at what had been the gangway's opening. The ropes and chains had been drawn and the ship had pushed away from the dock. He looked down at the widening gap of black water. He looked toward the colors all muted and hazy in the early moon's light. Francisco Golfinho leaned in and placed his hand on Manuel's shoulder. Manuel could smell the traces of after-shave and bacon fat mingling on Francisco's skin.

"Look at it," Manuel whispered. His eyes scanned the skyline. "It's like I want to . . . touch it, hold on to it."

"It's time to find our way back home." Francisco slapped Manuel's shoulder twice. Manuel thought of his mother. Over the months her face had softened in his mind. He thought of all the ways in which his siblings had suffered so much, had loved him unconditionally because they believed in their mother's fiction.

Francisco Golfinho moved his hand to the small of Manuel's back and Manuel reluctantly turned from the city. They were both caught by a mob of reveling men and Manuel staggered, then fell onto the ship's deck, where he choked on his disappointment, swallowed the snot in the back of his throat and wept.

It would be the final day of fishing before returning home. Manuel pushed off from the *Argus,* as he had done so many times before. But on this day he set the oars into the oarlocks and rowed out into the ocean's vastness with a renewed sense of vitality; he had seen a part of the world that seemed boundless and felt he must be part of it. With these thoughts swimming in his mind he drifted for hours in the dense fog. He could hear the voices of the other men singing as they fished, but no vision could pierce the wall of white mist. He tried to row in a certain direction but then realized there was no direction, no bearing.

The long days passed. Alone on his dory, Manuel gnawed at the bluish-white flesh of the cod he'd caught. Taste had abandoned him now and all that remained was his fear. During the day the sun pounded his head as he lay rocking on the dory's bottom. To cool his mind, Manuel remembered himself as a boy, diving into the waters every morning, burlap sac and a forged trident in hand. He would make his way to what he called the clam stone, a large rock formed by lava that flowed toward the shore, only to bubble into a solid black form millions of years ago. He would step onto its hollowed smoothness worn by sand, sea, and time. Manuel would pick at all the bounty trapped at low tide—*God's gift.* There was always the initial stab when he dove into the ocean. But then his eyes would adjust to the wonderful world of the green waters. He loved the feeling of his hair being free, individual strands swarming around his head. The sense of control: holding his breath till his lungs burned, kicking his way to the sun-drenched surface before taking in another deep breath and going under again. He would spear only what was necessary, only what they could eat that day. But before he left he would always mangle one of the smaller fish he had caught and make his way to the rocky bottom, dive down along the drop wall and gently

OF GOD AND COD

offer his hand and wiggle the bait, hoping the large black grouper would appear again. It never did.

It was a cold night when Manuel lay down flat on the bottom of the dory, made the sign of the cross and looked up at the stars. He thought of the dream he had sacrificed and all the things he would never know. And then he prayed. The dory rocked, lifted and twirled, a mere twig caught by the force and power of the ocean. The storm was building and Manuel knew that it was only a matter of time.

~

Frightened by the impenetrable dark, he breaks the surface, gasps and coughs up the crucifix. Salt water splashes against his face, forces his lips open, gushing in like an uninvited guest as he chokes on bile.

Don't panic—the panicked are dead.

His perfectly round face remains above water, then disappears under a small rolling wave, only to bob and break the surface again. Suddenly, there is nothing but ocean and a promising sky full of fading stars. The ocean has been lulled. The worst has passed. Manuel tilts his head back, ears submerged just under the waterline. He tries kicking his numb legs to propel himself into a back float—if only for a short while more. His burning arms and wrists circle in vain. He looks up at the sky, urging the sun to arrive and warm him. His heavy worn leather shoes were the first things to sink into the ocean's muddy depths. His wool pants followed, his childhood fishing belt sinking with them. But the fisherman's sweater, its pounds of soaked cabling, cannot be allowed to go, not just yet. He moves with the dancing waves. Only, he does not lead.

"Manuel," he hears a familiar voice call in singsong.

He recognizes the voice he has not heard in years.

"Big Lips, is that you?" Manuel says.

He sees the large grouper burst out of the water, its olive and grey shimmering body twisting over him in an arc. He thinks he sees the fish grinning at him with those balloon lips before its black-blotched shape plunges into the water without a splash.

"Big Lips. Come back!"

He waits, but hears only the lapping of water breaking under his chin. The sea invites him down once again. His arms no longer push through the water, his legs abandon him. Manuel Antonio Rebelo looks up at the new sun as he fills his lungs with air and slips once again under the surface, this time with eyes shut.

As he drops, he sees his father's smile, his mother's expression of betrayal, his abandoned brothers and sisters, and the women and children he will never know. He breathes out his last pocket of air, bubbles rising from him to pop on the surface. Manuel feels a tightening in his chest and arms, an inability to move and direct his weight. But instead of going down, his frame is tilting and twirling under the water's current. He feels himself dragged across and up, up toward the surface light. There is a gash of cold air before he feels the thud of his numb weight hitting a boat's wooden floor.

He adjusts his sight to see the face of a leathery man: toothless smile, uneven stubble, and half-soaked cigarette dangling from the corner of his mouth, cantilevered on his lip.

"Hmmm," is all the man grunts.

Manuel lies trembling on a nest of jumbled net. He grabs hold of the boat's edge, retching onto the wooden floor. There is a sense that he is not quite saved. He is thankful to lie curled, wound tightly in a ball as woollen blankets are draped over him. Every so often he squints at the back of a plaid woolen jacket, green rubber boots, and a man's piston arms, elbows pointing back, bringing the oars up with his hairy knuckles. Again and again. He falls in and out of an exhausted sleep.

"What do they call you, b'y, now?" the man asks.

"Manuel."

He had taken a few lessons in basic English before setting sail and had picked up more from the men on board the *Argus*. He learned everyday words—*house, girl, boy, food*—and phrases: "What is your name?" which required the proper response, "*My name is Manuel.*" But, the leathery man did not offer his name in return.

Manuel can only think of fresh water, food, and warmth. He can hear the mumbled questions this man is asking, but right now he is too spent to respond. All Manuel can do is think of home, his mother, the men of the *Argus,* and the news that will greet them all. Suddenly, a new, distant voice pierces his thoughts.

"Dad! Dad! Did you catch anything?" the echo travels.

Manuel struggles to lean up on his elbow and looks over the rim of the tiny boat for the first time. His eyes can only distinguish a girl's slight figure and the glint of sun radiating from her. She stands atop a glossy bed of kelp and runs her hands through her light brown hair, adjusts some strands behind her ears and tugs the hem of her flower-print skirt over her rubber boots. Manuel squints at a glare that flashes off her leg. The bottom of the boat scuffs onto land, tilts slightly to one side, then stops.

"Pepsi, my love. Your father caught you a big one."

He roars with laughter as he hauls the wet twine, heaves the bow of the boat farther up and carves into the pebbled shore.

"Been out to sea too long, but he's home now." He looks over his shoulder, then adjusts his voice to a whisper.

Manuel looks at his daughter; he can see she is absorbed by her father's "catch."

"He's some mother's boy, understand. We gotta take good care of him."

As her father busies himself with unloading the dory, the girl traces Manuel's lips with her index finger. Manuel struggles to keep his eyes open. He sees her clasping her hands together as if in prayer. She raises her chin to the sky exposing her long white neck. Manuel closes his eyes. As his mind retreats into a deep sleep he thinks he hears her mumble, "Thank you, Lord."

~ REASON TO BLAME ~

MANUEL'S EYELIDS FLUTTER when she lifts his head to give him water. It dribbles from the corners of his mouth, trickles down his chin and neck. Pepsi smiles when this happens, scrunches up her shoulders and giggles. She takes care of Manuel. When she thinks he's asleep she combs his hair, lightly outlines his eyebrows, and then moves down the bridge of his nose with her finger. Manuel senses her excitement in daring to hover her lips over his as he lies in his makeshift cot with his eyes closed. He grumbles something and snorts a bit. Pepsi thinks he is going to wake up, and moves quickly to the foot of his cot to slip her father's best socks onto Manuel's feet. She smiles. Her face is small, her hair is straight and divided by a long line of white scalp; each half falls down her face, hiding the corners of her eyes. She reaches into a bowl and unravels a steaming towel, which she drapes over his face. "Shhh. Close your eyes," she whispers. Manuel sinks back into the pillow. The heat of the towel makes his skin tingle, scalds as it surges up his nostrils and then lulls him momentarily. When she removes the cooling towel Manuel smiles. She pretends she does not notice. He sees her eyes darting quickly to the task at hand as she stretches his skin taut with her thumb and forefinger, then carefully shaves in the direction of his growth. Manuel's eyes move down her slender neck, down to her small breasts hidden beneath her sweater, then up again. Hers is not the sun-stained neck of a Portuguese girl. Manuel's knotted throat burns as the tears pool in his eyes.

"Shhh. It'll be all right. Pepsi's here, now. Shhh," she whispers in a singsong.

Cara Mãe,

I hope this letter reaches you. I'm alive! Weak, but saved. I've made it to my terra nova, lost for drowned but saved by a fisherman—a good man, Andrew. You always said that God's real messenger was the fisherman; well, he's mine and he's delivered me, taken me into his home.

When I left, there was so much that remained unsaid. Father's crucifix hangs from my neck still, lies close to my heart.

I feel certain about what it is I need to say, what it is you need to hear.

I always knew I didn't want to stay. I think you knew that also. I knew that if I stayed in our town, on our stifling island, I'd be consumed by what it was

you hoped and dreamed for me. Please understand,
Mãe. Don't be disappointed. I want to leave a mark
on this world, *Mãe*, and I know it's what you've always
wanted also. I need you to believe there is a place for
me here, a tomorrow. I'm certain of it and always
have been.

    Your loving son,
    Manuel

"You . . . ugly girl!" he roars as he stumbles in.

Manuel hears him from the main room. He tilts his
head back to see Pepsi getting out of her bed. She has
begun to leave her door open at night. Manuel sees her
struggle as she jackknifes her body, pivots, then swings
from under the covers her pink stump that ends just
below the knee. Her good leg dangles over the edge of the
bed. She squints his way; it's dark and her eyes haven't
adjusted well enough to know if he's seen her. She reaches
for her wooden leg, the one she has outgrown, that rests
on the floor next to her chamber pot. Her hands blur as
they weave the leather straps and secure the metal brace to
her thigh—the molded cup meets the hardened flesh
where her leg should be. He's not sure how he feels about
it—she is not whole. But, when she brushes by him he is
caught in her smell of cotton sheets and the peppered
sweetness of cinnamon. There is intrigue in her
difference—something fragile that needs his tending.
Manuel wants to hold her, touch her.

Pepsi meets her father at the front door. He loses his
balance and tries to grab on to the wall. It's not enough.

She's there to direct the running fall toward his bedroom, where he flops onto his bed. Manuel tries to get up and help but then falls back against his pillow. She struggles with Andrew's coat and kneads him like dough, gaining momentum to flip him over onto his back. Manuel can smell him from where he is: beer, stale piss, the spice of tobacco in damp wool, the flakes of a fish pie always evident on his stubbly chin and cardigan. Pepsi looks back again to see if Manuel is awake. He moves up to rest on his forearm. He wants to help her. She waves him off and hauls her father's boots from his feet and then threadbare socks before hoisting his legs up onto the mattress and pulling the covers under his chin. Manuel has made it to Andrew's room, leaning against the door frame.

"Thank the Lord you won't be runnin' away like your mother." Andrew cups her face with his hand and brushes her lips with his sausage-like thumb. Unnoticed by him, she spits his fingers away.

"You're my . . . my sweet ugly girl. And a wooden leg to boot."

He smiles when he whispers these words, breathes out his judgment. His body now relaxes, his weight molding itself to the mattress as he sinks into a drunken sleep, mouth wide open.

She comes out of his room. "Go to sleep, Manuel. I'll take care of things."

Manuel moves back to the cot, urged by her hand on the small of his back. She turns on the tap. The gush of water splatters against the cement basin. She finds the empty Javex bottle hidden in the cabinet under the sink and grabs a wooden spatula. She moves past Manuel into her father's room. She kneels before his sleeping lump, pulls back the covers and undoes his zipper. She looks away and with the spatula fishes for his penis, and expertly aims it into the neck of the jug. A good couple of taps on the hollow plastic jug wakes him just enough to hear the running water. It's all that's needed—the hot, cloudy pee trickles, then gurgles into the bottle.

Cara Mãe,

Every day I get stronger. Andrew and his daughter, Pepsi, are taking good care of me. They ask for nothing. I want to help, to show them my gratitude. There are so many stories to tell . . . of the big ship, its men, how I was swallowed by the sea, of St. John's and its streets and people . . . I hope you have received my gifts that I mailed to you while in St. John's. I pray that you got my first letter before the black news that must have greeted you from the commander of the fleet.

You were visited fifteen years ago with news of our dear father's death; the idea that you and all my brothers and sisters would hear those same words fall from the mouth of an unknown man pains me. But I am alive, *Mãe,* and this must give you some comfort.

Please don't see this decision I have made as a rejection of the promise you saw in me. I will work hard to show you that it still burns inside me, brighter than ever.

Every time I breathe in the brackish mist, it reminds me of home. The new land is far, and even though it smells just like home, I find that now I can breathe. I don't know why I want you to know this other than a month has passed and the November winds here are building, getting colder and forceful, and I have yet to hear a word from you.

Please don't be angry with me. You have my brothers and sisters to look after. Love them as I do.

Your son,
Manuel

"Plucked outta the water, my boy."

The days are punctuated by Andrew's repeated boast. He puffs himself up like he's caught a prize fish and they're going to take his picture for the local newspaper. Manuel cannot help but smile with gratitude at his outbursts.

Manuel is feeling strong enough to help Andrew skin the animals that he has hunted and trapped: rabbits, deer, and an ugly animal Andrew calls moose. Manuel has made the job easier by driving some large rusty hooks into the trunk of an old tree out back. He shows Andrew, mostly with exaggerated gestures, how to tie the legs of the dead animal together with rope, loop the rope through the eyehook and then the pulley to drag and hoist the carcass against the tree. The animal's body stretches and drapes toward the ground and Manuel's sharp knife cuts into its flesh, thinly separating the hide from that milky blue membrane that encases the meat.

Every so often, Manuel cannot help but gaze at the naked cabin through the curtain of steam that rises from the animal. The oxblood paint flakes along its planked sides. Two small windows jut out slightly in the front and the black narrow door sits crooked on its hinges. The wind has ravaged the bleak little house that sits on the grassy hill. But all Manuel can think of is the warmth and comfort within those walls and sagging roof. On a few occasions, he has caught Pepsi looking out the window. She always turns away in time. It's all play and it makes him want her more.

Earlier, that morning, Manuel had been roused from his sleep by Pepsi's excited giggles. "Wake up, Manuel. Come see." Somewhat groggy, Manuel lumbered half-naked to the front door and stepped outside. Snowflakes, large and generous, fell languidly from the sky in silence. They fell on Manuel's hair and lashes, his bare shoulders and feet, where they disappeared into the heat of his skin. Manuel raised his hands, tried to catch the flakes between his fingers. Bewildered, he turned toward the house. Pepsi squatted in the doorway, held her robe's sleeve in her mouth. Manuel had twirled like a boy, raised his head to the snow's newness, opened his mouth and flicked his tongue.

"You better watch yourself, young lady," Andrew says as he and Manuel return to the house. Pepsi continues to stare out the window as if she has not heard him.

"That man's not for you. A good strong man needs a good woman to make him a life, you hear?"

Manuel has grown quite used to them talking about him as if he doesn't understand a word. Truth be told, he doesn't understand *many* of the words, but he is clear about the passion behind these foreign sounds.

"I prayed for him, though. He's for me. He's the answer," her whisper fades.

There are times when Manuel notices the fear in Andrew's eyes. At other times, he's embarrassed by Andrew's mocking.

"You stupid girl . . . there is no answer. Look at you." He shakes his head as he walks out the front door.

Before she can react, Manuel moves toward the sink to rinse his bloodstained hands. Duty washes over her; she confidently grabs his hands and scrubs them. She doesn't look at him. Manuel allows her to scour his hands with a brush. They begin to burn in their rawness but he doesn't draw them back. It helps to let her father's words wash away with the blood and grime; they swirl in the basin and lose themselves in the drain. Her neck begins to relax; she turns to face him and her mouth smiles but her eyes betray her. Manuel lets her clean under his nails. He buries his nose in her hair, breathes in and moves into her warmth. She nudges his head a bit and her shoulders drop. Manuel can hear her exhale. He doesn't care about her leg.

Cara Mãe,

I still have not heard from you. Your refusal to send me a letter only adds to the heaviness that weighs in my heart. It has taken hold of my mind.

I am growing fond of this girl, Pepsi. She is six-teen but already a woman of work, just like the girls back home. I know you'd like her, *Mãe*, the same way you liked Silvia before she left to go to school in the city. But, there is something about this girl, Pepsi; she makes all of my plans for this new land seem right, even real. I'm capable of taking hold of my dreams and moving on with my new life.

You used to say that the young don't know what they want. I am not so fragile as to believe that anymore. I'm a man, not a boy. The worth of things in life comes with risk. You taught me that. There is no doubt in my mind that my decision was the right one. Please have faith in me; you always have.

Send something soon, *Mãe*. Let me know if you are all well. My strength is with me, now.

Your son,
Manuel

Manuel has asked Pepsi to mail the letters he's written, all addressed to São Miguel, Açores. Pepsi asks who Maria Theresa da Conceição Rebelo is. She looks relieved when Manuel tells her. He wonders what his mother must be thinking now—if she even knows. It's been weeks; has she received word yet that her son has met his father's same fate—lost at sea? Or, could his letters have reached her first, saving her from this torment. Or after, with news of a resurrection? He is eager for a response.

"Fishermen need to live by the sea, don't they, Manuel?"

"Yes, Andrew," Manuel nods.

Andrew begins to dress in layers of coats and then tops off his head with a hat, the fur-lined flaps framing his ruddy face. He is off to check his traps. His padded frame can barely fit through the narrow door. As he hunkers down to go out he turns to look at Manuel, who is writing a letter, and then quickly moves to look at his daughter, who lifts a heavy roasting pan out of the oven in a billow of steam and brushes her wet bangs away from her face with her forearm. He grunts as he moves out the door like a lumbering bear.

"My father told me we have to keep quiet about this or they'll send you to some farm in Ontario, Manuel . . . to work."

"Is okay, Pepsi. Shhh. I no say nothing." Manuel picks at her loose hair and tucks some strands behind her ears.

"I don't want anyone to know, Manuel." They both sit on Manuel's cot.

"No one."

"I don't know why she left. I thought it was me, or more her disappointment in giving birth to me? It was all too much for her, I suppose. Growing up I wanted to know—I wanted a reason to blame. Do you understand, my darling?"

Manuel didn't ask the question about her mother, although he had often wondered. She had been seven when her mother left her, them. Her father never made much sense when he tried to explain. But in his lame drunken attempts, deep down Pepsi knew *he* was the reason.

"*This barren heath*—that's what she called this place; it's too far from Brigus to be called anything. But this was the place where she gave birth to me, alone. And as the years passed I began to notice the sadness in her eyes. Maybe she wanted a reason to blame too."

Pepsi fixes her eyes on the front doorknob and talks. She looks up at Manuel to see if he is listening.

"I guess I'll never know."

"You father no say why?"

"Ah, whatever Father tried to do to reassure my mother was never enough, though. A child can see things, you know, Manuel."

"Is hard for lose a mother. But memories you have, no? This make you strong. It make *me* strong."

She smiles at Manuel's much-improved conversation. She is tired and flushed but happy to keep going.

She tells Manuel of her yearly birthday trip to St. John's where, if need be, she would get fitted for a new leg and brace. She swings her head from side to side with each memory: the smells of her mother's cooking, the hours her mother spent teaching her to read, the little dog her mother had left behind who ran after a blowing leaf then disappeared over the cliff. Pepsi rushed to the edge and saw his body smashed and crooked against the shore rocks.

"All I have left of my mother is this strand of almost-pink pearls she bought for me at a place called Kresge's, in Toronto—that's what the box said. She sent them to me on my tenth birthday along with a note: *Dear Pepsi, Please don't be angry. I just couldn't any longer. I needed to breathe.*" She rolls her fingertips along the necklace.

Manuel wants to kiss her.

"It wasn't even signed and it was all she ever sent me. I don't even know what my mother's signature looks like, but I'm certain her *L* for Lucille is looped both on the top and bottom, big loops." She draws the letter with its curlicues in the air like a child.

Cara Mãe,

You have not written. I know you are angry but I need to know that you understand.

Pepsi has no mother. Life hasn't been easy for her but she's strong. She's what I've always wanted.

Mãe, remember when Jose brought that calf home, the one we had to tear from its mother's belly? He brought that calf through the front door . . . you yelled at him, struck him. He nursed it back; he slept in that barn for weeks, fed it milk in a bottle until it was strong and ready. You thought he was afraid to come back. But you were wrong, *Mãe*. He stayed in that barn because there was purpose for him, something to care for. It made him strong. It made me strong.

It's not your fault. I don't write this to hurt you—you are my mother and I love you. But I needed a purpose too.

I know you are disappointed in these words but I am not angry or bitter. The life you gave me was a gift but it is mine and I must cherish it. Please understand.

Manuel

"I no think I go, Andrew."

Pepsi trips against the bench as she clears the table. They both look at Manuel.

"Well . . . guess you should rest up awhile longer." Andrew speaks to Manuel but follows Pepsi, tries to lock his eyes with hers.

Pepsi goes into her room and busies herself with folding the laundry, not looking as her father leaves the house. She turns to see Manuel scanning her body, moving down to her legs, where his eyes stop. He knows she is uncomfortable with his stare but he can't seem to tear himself away. Manuel's glare is snapped by Andrew's shadow as it moves across her window. It will be a long walk to Brigus, via crooked roads and barren fields of rock toward his weekly night in town. Pepsi moves to shut her bedroom door.

"Pepsi?"

Manuel loves the way her name sounds. He rests his forehead against her door. She hasn't shut it in weeks. He waits a little longer before calling out again, and taps at the door.

"Pepsi?"

"Come in," and as quickly as the words roll off her tongue, Manuel opens the door and can see that she is nervous. She is fidgeting with the pleats of her skirt. She sits now at the edge of her bed looking out. At night, Manuel has caught her sitting in the same spot, rubbing oil of wintergreen—its familiar fresh scent was used to massage Manuel's joints—around her hardened stump, preparing it for the next day's pounding and grinding. Now, she just sits there, back straight, silently looking out the window. She moves the blanket over her leg. Manuel moves behind her small frame and runs a hand along her hair and down her neck. She catches his hand with her cheek and traps it there. Manuel sits beside her and moves his free hand under the blanket. She is tense but when she kisses his knuckles that rest in the crook of her neck, Manuel takes it as a sign, an invitation. His hand moves along her wooden leg then touches her brace—a tangle of warm wood and cold metal. Her back tenses. He doesn't flinch. His other hand dislodges from her neck and shoulder and he cups her smallish face, forces her pleading eyes to meet his. Manuel drags the back of his hand down over the raised grain of the wooden shin. He kisses her papery eyelids. His hand flips over and his fingertips continue up her leg, traversing the stainless steel bridgework, up, up toward her inner thigh. She looks at him, her silence invites him further. He moves his hand down again and wedges a finger between the wooden leg and her worn stump. He nestles it there and feels a strange exhilaration. She pulls at her skirt, tries to cover her shame.

"Shhh . . . Manuel no hurt Pepsi."

She closes her eyes and feels his fingers on her brace, as if he made it flesh.

Cara Mãe,

I will continue to write in the hope that these letters will somehow make their way into your heart. You've never felt anything like it. In one day there can be a downpour of rain, blustering snow, and sunshine.

The snow is quite nice but it's so cold. Andrew says it gets so cold your pee can freeze.

I'm sure you're preparing for Christmas, *Mãe*. I miss the smell of pine crushed beneath our feet, sweet masa, and the smell of our home in the damp night. I hope my siblings are all well. I can still picture them in my mind but I'm certain so much has changed. Please tell them I miss them.

Laughter is returning to this house. It lives in this country, I know. A house needs laughter.

I hope that when Albina reads these letters to you that you are not angry. Please write or let Jose or Candida write something . . . I long to hear from someone.

Albina, write something. Please let me know how all my news and thoughts are being received. She need not know.

Merry Christmas.
Manuel

He doesn't want to think back. Although his heart aches for the familiar, he needs to look forward. There is a merciless rattle in his brain: It was fate that tossed him into the sea, alone and lost; it was fate that hooked him onto the line of a fisherman; it must then be fate that made Manuel turn up to that dove-gray sky that always visits after a storm—look up at the heavens only to find Pepsi. He will not tempt that fate. She has been good to him, nursed him and loved him. Manuel owes it to her to love her back.

"Pepsi!" Andrew's voice stabs through Manuel's thoughts. "Where are my pants?" he shouts from his room.

"They were reekin' of screech, soiled to the grain. So I washed them."

Pepsi has found a new confidence and strength. Andrew storms in from his room. Pepsi's eyes do not leave her father's. She will not let him win. He can't say anything for the longest time. Pepsi hums as she trusses the bird.

"That's what it's about, Manuel. Mark my words. You give them everything they could ever ask for only to have them walk on you like the dirt they think you are."

"Dad, I didn't—"

"Don't you 'Dad' me. Respect!" he sputters. "It's all I've ever asked of you in this house. Respect!" He struggles to put on his coat, then goes out and slams the door.

Manuel moves recklessly behind her, kisses her neck.

"Tell me, Pepsi—tell about that day." It is his favorite story. It is filled with everything he wants in life: beginning with sacrifice and ending with hope and promise. Manuel digs his hands under the neckline of her dress, holds the weight of her breasts.

"Well," she begins, welcoming the distraction, "that day . . ." Pepsi turns and smiles before continuing. "That day, I was coming home from St. John's where I stupidly thought I could sell my pearls. I thought I could get enough money to get my hair done at a salon and maybe buy a pretty dress. A girl likes a pretty dress, Manuel. That lady at the pawnshop sat there in her stool behind the counter looking at her large black and white television. She saw me from the corner of her eye and pretended not to notice. I laid my pearls gently on top of the glass display. She bit one of the pearls with her graying teeth and showed me its plastic core, dropped the string of pearls back on the counter, *clickety-click,* all the while looking up at her television, and resumed tapping her fingers on the counter to our pet Juliette—a girl with a beautiful voice and perky smile. You'd like her, Manuel . . ."

Manuel rubs her hardening nipple between his thumb and forefinger. She is comfortable with the way his calloused hands move across her body. When she turns her face to kiss him, she no longer looks awkward, afraid.

"Manuel, let me finish the story."

He knows she doesn't want him to stop and he knows the end of the story; the lady had made a mistake. The pearls were real. Her mother gave them to her. How she prayed during the bus ride home, prayed to all the saints in heaven. *Please, Jesus, give me a new leg—flesh and bone . . .* How she imagined her leg growing, a ticklish tingling, and then, her final prayer: *Dear Lord, please give me a man—a family to take care of.*

"That very next morning, like every other morning, I went down to the shore to meet my father. When I saw him rowing in toward the shallows, his boat cutting through the foam, I saw that he'd brought me a gift richer than a new leg or real pearls—he'd brought me you." She breathes out her last words, then playfully whips his face with the damp tea towel.

Cara Mãe,

I'm writing this on the eve of Christmas. It is now two full months and I must beg your forgiveness. Is this why you have not written? Or is it because I have made it clear I have no plans of returning? Before I left I told you that our small island held nothing for me. I still believe this to be true. What is it, *Mãe?* Tell me.

I find myself exhausted by the pace at which the images of life back home run across my mind: growing up as a boy, patches of green fields and beds of calla lily, Gilberto—our toothless dog, my brown-eyed siblings, your hard-working hands against your black dress and veil. And then in a wave I think of my pressed cotton shirts and new leather shoes with their tight shoelaces, windows that would not open, houses too narrow. I gulp for air but there is nothing but chalk and dust. But these are my images, my burdens. Believe me when I say I do not blame you, *Mãe.*

My thoughts are with you all this Christmas.

Manuel

The day begins filled with the joy and promise that only Christmas can bring. Pepsi has gotten up early to get everything done: the chicken is stuffed, the dough is pounded into plump balls and allowed to rise in the kitchen's heat. Manuel imagines he is in his own little house, not Andrew's. Children are playing around the tinseled tree, a girl and a boy. They're trying to peek at their presents. Manuel is looking through the window outside. Pepsi is cooking up a wonderful meal, stuffing and roast potatoes with *chouriço*, and she's making his favorite cod dish to remind him of home. Manuel walks in, twirls his daughter then throws the boy high into the air and catches the giggling copy of himself securely in his arms . . .

"Manuel, Father didn't come home last night. Do you know where he got to?"

"I go look for him, Pepsi. You no worry."

Manuel circles the fields, then runs to the cliffs to see if there is any unfortunate evidence. For hours he looks along the coast, down toward the foamy cove, then scans the landscape. He does not want to go back empty handed. He returns only to hear some muffled shouts coming from inside the shed. Andrew is curled around an empty jug. He looks up and shields his eyes from the white sky. He then smiles at Manuel. It has been a while since Andrew has smiled at Manuel in that way. It feels good.

Manuel drapes Andrew over his shoulder like the animals he drags to the tree. Andrew is much larger than Manuel, big and heavy. Manuel manages to drop him into his chair. Pepsi slams a lid onto the counter. Andrew struggles but cannot pull himself up to the table.

"Everything is cold," she says. The candles have burned down to nothing.

"*Feliz Natal*, Andrew." Manuel smiles.

Pepsi decides not to ruin the day further. "Dad, will you cut the bird now?" she asks.

"Why don't you ask the man of the house?" he slurs.

His words are filled with bitterness. Manuel pretends they have not hurt him. Pepsi is about to say something until her father breaks in: "I have a gift for you, Manuel."

Manuel looks to Pepsi, who twists her hair into tight ringlets.

"Dad, please don't embarrass me." She struggles to get up. "Please don't do this to me."

"Shush!" He pounds the table with his knotted fist. Pepsi tries to push herself away but Andrew pins her small hand firmly against the tabletop. She lowers herself back onto her chair and sits hunched over. Her eyes dart across the room then up to the wooden beams before she drops her chin against her breastbone. "This is still my house, though, and I want to say something."

He narrows his eyes at Manuel as if daring him to a challenge.

"Manuel. We have taken you in and treated you like family."

Manuel lowers his head, ready for his censure.

"You well know no man could'uv done more for you. It's time you made plans, I'd say."

With these words he lifts himself from his chair and half stumbles toward the Christmas tree. He falls to the floor, where he clumsily searches for a gift. He crawls back to the table with a smug grin. The present he clutches is wrapped in the brown paper used to wrap meat at the butcher's. There are smeared traces of blood on the parchment. He flings the packet across the table as he pulls himself up and takes his seat.

"Thank you, Andrew." Manuel is unsure of the offering. "I bless by you . . . and Pepsi. Thank you."

Manuel begins to work his fingers around the package. He glances up, expecting to meet Pepsi's gaze. He's confused by the way she stares at his hands unraveling the string, flipping the gift over before lifting the center fold. Her eyes look at nothing else. In a split second his letters slip from his hands and fan themselves on the table.

The room begins to spin. Manuel glimpses the smirk on Andrew's face, the tree, the perfectly browned chicken sitting in the middle of the set table, gleaming plates and flickering candles. The images swarm in his head. Bile rises from his stomach, sharp and sour. Then he sees Pepsi getting up and tripping over her lifeless leg. She cannot look at him. She falls down and drags herself the rest of the way across the floor. She reaches her threshold, pushes the door open with her shoulder and is swallowed by the dark mouth of her room. Manuel sits still and numb. The door closes. He hears the click of the lock and the din of his own silence over her father's simmering laughter.

~ FADO ~

My boat skipped across the surface
of the great wide sea,
so angry and cruel.
Yet, I danced and sang and smiled,
tempted by the comfort
of my mind's dream.
I will not stop my little boat
from skipping across the sea.
I will dance, sing, and live,
but only live my dream for me . . .

WITH ANGUISH, MATEUS ALMEIDA sings a fado, while
his guests sit at his table and weep. Manuel's ass leans
against the edge of the counter. He wipes the glass with
the tea towel, Mateus's "No spots" chiming in his head.
Mateus hired Manuel to do odd jobs in his boarding

house, and Manuel is grateful to him. At fifty, Mateus is immaculate in every way: he cuts a fine silhouette in his tailored clothes, his greased hair, and buffed nails; the way he turns down a bed, dipping his hands in a small bowl of warm water, flicking the excess before smoothing the lip of the downturned sheets with his moistened palm creating a sharp crease. "We were not born here, Manuel. You must always appear to be . . . more," he says without a hint of superiority. The truth is Mateus can't walk down to the harbor without men lifting their hats to him, even the bank manager who sits behind a desk with the glittering pocket watch and cauliflower nose. The women silently swoon as the children chase him like swarming hornets until he is forced to toss a nickel in the air, allowing enough time to get away.

"Remember this, Manuel: they *almost* think I am one of them. But, they never do . . . not completely."

Mateus Almeida hangs on to the final note with his eyes closed. The young moths ping against the lightbulb that dangles, caught in a cloud of smoke, over the kitchen table. There is a reverent quiet as Mateus lays down his *guitarra.* Then Eduardo's tobacco-stained teeth appear as he begins to clap. His friend Duarte begins to clap too, and soon it builds to a crescendo of clapping, grunting, and laughter. Mateus smiles and raises his hands in thanks. He pours the men another glass of *vinho.* The sailors are from the *Gil Eannes,* which came through the Narrows and entered the harbor of St. John's that morning. Over the next two days, while the fishermen and all of St. John's prepare for the city's festivities, Mateus's boarding house will be home to some of them.

"Manuel, come here," he motions with his arm.

Manuel leaves the few remaining dishes to soak in the sink. "Yes, Senhor Mateus." Apart from cleanliness, it is the only other condition Mateus insists on; there is to be nothing other than English spoken between them in his house. Mateus insists it is the only way to be a success in this country.

"Are the rooms ready for these men?"

"I make them ready this morning."

"I prepared them this morning. P-r-e-p-a-r-e-d." He looks at Manuel and is quite pleased to hear his pupil softly utter the word and phrase a couple of times to himself.

"Good. Now I'll play my *guitarra*—you sing."

"I no sing fado."

"Are you Portuguese?" Duarte holds Manuel with his rodent-like eyes. "*Açoreano?*"

Mateus picks up his instrument again. It is Manuel's cue to leave—he notices the twitch of Mateus's L-shaped sideburns that thin to a pencil point before meeting his perfectly trimmed mustache—and he moves down the corridor. Mateus knows the story, how Manuel was left for drowned and that he was saved by a fisherman and his daughter. He also knows of the betrayal by the girl called Pepsi. He smiled when Manuel told him. It had angered Manuel to have his notion of love met with laughter. Until Mateus came home the next day with a coffee-colored liquid inside a bottle; *Pepsi-Cola,* the label read. Manuel tasted it and didn't like it very much, too sweet. They had both smiled. Mateus knows of the struggle, how Manuel worked his way down the tiny outports dotting Conception Bay until, somewhat exhausted and disillusioned, he settled in St. John's and into Mateus's home on the corner of Duckworth and Cathedral streets.

Manuel does not have the security of official papers and it is best that no one else knows he is here. The commander of the *Gil Eannes*—Portugal's official representative in the North Atlantic—is in St. John's. He is powerful, respected, and feared. Unlike some, he does not derive pleasure from the challenge of making the crooked straight. That is work. What he reveres is maintenance and control. The idea that Manuel drowned, his bloated body never skimmed from the sea's frothy surface, is a blemish on his record. Even though he was not the *Argus*'s captain, he was responsible for all of the men signed to the White Fleet.

After five months Manuel's room remains uncluttered, empty of anything that is his. There are a dozen or so letters addressed to his mother that may never be mailed. Manuel is uncertain of what it is he wants to say to her, whether he wants to remain. The letters were written at a time when the world lay sprawled in front of him, so full of hope and promise. He still wears his father's gold crucifix and his old fisherman's sweater. There is a single bed with a patchwork quilt, a simple night table (the drawer doesn't open), an infuriating small lamp with a yellowing shade that he tilts to stop the bulb from flickering, a chipped stand-up ashtray, and a strong wooden chair—the last two things he drags every night to his window for a cigarette. Manuel doesn't want to own anything—to feel the burden of having to care for things. He's young. He wants to be able to pick up and leave, go anytime.

Manuel can hear the tinkling of Mateus's *guitarra;* his trembling vocals spill over from the kitchen window. Mateus never knew his father. At least Manuel has an image of his father firmly imprinted in his head that occasionally flings itself to the forefront of his thoughts. Mateus is certain his father was a fisherman, convinced he was lost at sea. His mother was a fishmonger in the open market in Lisbon; she never said much. Mateus is always there to greet the men of the White Fleet as they get off their ships. "They've been out for so long, so alone. We're their family, now," he says. Manuel believes that it is more of a hope—that Mateus will one day see his father step out onto the dock, out into the glaring sun, reclaimed.

Manuel's room is on the top floor of the four-story house. He looks out his bay window, down toward the black harbor. It was last year that he had stepped off the great fishing vessel *Argus* and onto the dock to gaze at the wood-clad buildings and the twin towers of the church looming over this city. He looked upon the bustling port with slit eyes and grinned with wonder, delight. Now he thinks of his struggle to get back here. Manuel doubts if there is still a place for him in this Terra Nova, if his dream is worth holding on to.

He remembers the bitter night he left Pepsi in her little house on the hill, how the snow began to fall the very moment he stepped out the front door with a bundle on his back. He could see Brigus in the distance, a grouping of pinprick lights piercing the dark. He thought he would be able to find work there, but there would be no work for a fisherman in December.

The next morning he came upon a sign, EAST COAST ROPE AND LINE, and attempted to open the door. Everything was locked and an eerie solitude lay among the small cluster of homes scattered in the distance.

He spent another night in an open shed behind the factory. The next day he was hired by a short man with no neck. Manuel was instructed to call him Mr. Johnson. He lasted three days working for this brutish little man who waddled along the factory aisle between fishermen, unsympathetic to their yearnings for the familiar roar of the sea. Manuel cut his hands as he guided the jute onto spools that spun wildly atop metal rods. When he could bear it no longer he took the money he was reluctantly offered and moved again. As long as he kept moving in the direction of St. John's, he thought.

A couple days later he found himself in a smaller town where he met a few men who had gathered near a dock and who magically seemed to repel the splashing ocean that crashed against the concrete breaker. They were all dressed in tattered costumes, some in women's garb. One of the men held a mask between his knees, the others had tied their veils around their necks. Manuel knew about these men who would wander from village to village at night, playing the fool with their ceremonial knocks. In Portugal, the new year always began with church and then a night of wild revelry. There was dancing and drinking, all disguised while greeting neighbors with "*boas festas!*" Manuel was warmed by these recollections of boyhood, dashing through the small village singing old songs called *janeiras*. Once their true identities were guessed correctly the children were required to "unveil" and were rewarded with food or coins.

A few days later he found himself in a town with no name. Feeling abandoned, he turned about for some sense of direction. He was lost. A car passed by and stopped. The red curly hair and freckled face of a young man popped out the window. His name was Jack and he was on his way to St. John's and just wanted someone to talk to. "A man gets lonely," he said. "That's why I'm searching for something more, understand? Something that ain't going to be found on this here rock. Ontario's where I'm goin' to get me a future." He shouted his conversation as if he were speaking over loud music. Manuel listened and nodded, grateful that he was warm and in the company of a good soul.

> *. . . Parched in my desert of loneliness.*
> *Nothing left.*
> *Bread, bitter and dry,*
> *is what I'm given for food.*
> *I need nothing more.*
> *Hope is my only companion.*
> *Let me eat my bread*
> *which I will moisten with wine . . .*

Mateus's voice is tiring. They will all be in bed soon. Manuel's eyes land upon the men near the docks wearing mining lights strapped to their foreheads, casting their intersecting beams. That morning he looked down to the sea, to the piers in the harbor and the schooners of the

White Fleet. He had scanned the Battery to the west of
him, the gray flat flakes cutting horizontal lines against the
rusty cliffsides. He saw them on the docks beginning to lay
the large square frame made of mashed ferns and bound
with twine. They will work through the night decorating
the posts along the streets of St. John's with garlands of
pine and cedar. It would certainly be a relief from the
smell of fish and oil that wafted over the course of the day.
The roads will be paved with colorful petals that mark the
processional route. It is at this moment, with Mateus's
fado as a backdrop, that Manuel's heart longs for home.

> . . . But I will come to you.
> The early promise
> awakened by the sea
> is now hidden in a mist of fear
> of being alone . . .

It is a beautiful May morning. The crowds are beginning
to trickle in, appearing around the corners and clump-
ing along the roads that move from the wharves to the
gates of St. John the Baptist Church set high on the ridge.
Mateus has tried unsuccessfully to convince Manuel to
attend mass with him on Sundays. He never pushes.
There are too many scars . . . *those who serve me, serve God . . .
it's between us and God, understand?* The priest's voice still
haunts him.

The city is alive with a flurry of activity. Men scurry
up poles like mice to connect loudspeakers. Earlier, the
people of St. John's, to be drawn into the celebration,
had been asked by an ad in *The Telegram* to decorate their

homes and other buildings along the route. Wanting everyone to join in the festivities, parishioners knocked on the doors that lined the processional route, handing out colorful scrolls of silk to unfurl from their windows. The statue of *Nossa Senhora de Fátima,* Portugal's gift of friendship, will be carried up to the church to receive a solemn benediction, then set up for temporary display before being placed in the carefully prepared alcove for idol worship.

Many of the Portuguese fishermen are working in hurried preparation. A small cluster of four is standing on the corner, directly underneath Manuel's window. Their torsos disappear into burlap sacks and then reappear with greedy arms full of petals. Pink and blue hydrangea, scarlet dahlias, pale peonies, and golden sunflowers are slightly faded from the journey. The four men fill the geometric shapes within the frame with swatches of color, water the petals to weigh them down and prevent them from being blown away, then lift the large eight-by-eight template, careful not to disturb the stained glass–like mural that remains on the ground. Again, they tumble the frame over, dive into their burlap sacks, arms and fists full of petals to complete the next eight feet of fragile tapestry. They are working up the steep slope of Cathedral Street and will reach the church by noon, in time for the start of the procession.

Manuel curls back in bed, brings his knees up to his chest. He can taste the ache. He thinks of his own island, sees the excited women gathered outside their homes during the town's *festa* honoring *Nossa Senhora do Rosário,* decorating the street outside their stretch of windows in the same way. He wants to hear his mother's voice, yelling at his sisters to raise the wooden frame carefully so as not to disturb the flowers and to ensure perfection—"God sees everything," she'd say. And behind the front door, in the dark and cool recesses of their sun-drenched houses, he and his brothers, along with the men in the village, would pray by raising their shot glasses of *agua ardente*, before toppling them into their gullets with squints, a flush of red, a horsey snort, and a grin.

> *I came to harvest*
> *the greatness of the sea,*
> *and stormy winds did blow.*
> *The heavens above closed, roared their anger*
> *in dismal gloom.*
> *Mother, weep for your cherished son.*
> *Your wails carry across*
> *blasting waves, trumpeting gales.*
> *We must endure.*
> *The old ways remain;*
> *new hopes are crushed by jagged rocks*
> *of the mind . . .*

"Manuel. Wake up. Manuel." Mateus's thin mustache hovers over Manuel's face. "We're going to miss the parade." He smiles, exposing the large gap between his teeth. He motions for Manuel to take a seat with him by the window.

Mateus has taken the liberty of setting up the space for a celebration. The nightstand has been dragged next to the window. A boxed record player sits atop it. A black-and-white album cover of Amalia Rodrigues looking up to the sky leans against the crank. A few bottles of wine, two cups, and an ashtray sit on the sill. Manuel can hear the buzz of crowds gathered under the window.

"Come, Manuel."

"I . . . I must have fallen asleep, Mateus."

"It's okay. Your head is filled with too many thoughts."

"No, it's not like that."

"Manuel, I know . . . I can see."

Mateus had stowed away in the hull of one of the White Fleet's ships almost forty years ago. He had made a place for himself here. At first it had been difficult, a boy lost in an unknown, faraway place, not certain of what to do next. Repairing fishing nets had shredded his hands but fed his body. He had grown up on the docks, moved up in a world where there was promise of reward in hard work and perseverance. This was the dream of this land. Manuel wanted it to become his.

"You're young, Manuel. At twenty-one you have everything ahead of you."

"Then why do I feel I have nothing?" Manuel wants Mateus to turn and look his way, to answer the question. Instead, he turns the crank and places the album on the turntable. The record wobbles slightly. Amalia's voice erupts as Mateus's eyes urge Manuel to look out the window.

The thousands of men are moving up the street in step with Amalia's painful cries. The long floral carpet winds through the city streets. Thousands more have lined the roads to see the pageantry and to catch a glimpse of "the gift." Manuel is certain they have scrubbed themselves with cold seawater and large bars of glycerin soap. All of them—even those with curly and kinked hair—have their hair parted, greased flat, so that in the afternoon sun their heads look like glistening watermelon seeds. Manuel cannot help but grin.

"It's nice to see you smile, Manuel . . . a man who truly has nothing doesn't smile.

"Manuel. Listen to me . . ." It is his erect posture, straight like a mast, that tells Manuel he must listen. Mateus doesn't want Manuel to look at him; they will have the conversation, side by side, looking out the window.

"Don't let the *idea*," his strained neck stresses this word, "of a dream conquer you, Manuel. If you are going to stay . . . if you are going to *fazer uma América,* as many of these men say," he makes a tight ball with his fist. "Let this country shape *you.*"

"Can you mail some letters for me, Mateus?"

Mateus does not answer. He gets up, fills their glasses of wine to the brim, reaches to his side to crank the record player again and then leans out the window. His crisp white shirt billows in the spring breeze.

"Here she comes," he smiles.

The wave of men are outside their window now, somberly walking in uniform step. Some of them look up to catch the bittersweet longing in Amalia's voice. Some smile, others casually salute Mateus. Many have stayed with him before—their home away from home. In the near distance floats the four-foot-high statue of *Nossa Senhora do Fátima,* her floor-length veils topped with a silver crown. The twelve chosen carry her proudly on their shoulders. They move her slowly up the road, their steps soft. The statue is held tightly in place by wooden brackets covered with crimson velvet. It's clear the men know of the steep inclines on the route to the basilica.

A plump woman raises her stringy daughter above her head and onto her shoulders. This is her chance to see the Holy Mother, the gift that Portugal sent with its fishermen to commemorate a relationship that has lasted more than four hundred years.

"She's so small." Manuel hears the little girl say this amid the approaching hum of a band. *So young to be disappointed,* he thinks. *Nossa Senhora* stands on her crushed-velvet base looking sadly down at the three shepherd children that kneel at her feet. They too are part of the statue, but only their necks poke through the mound of flowers as the crowd continues to pelt her with daisies and carnations as the men turn the corner and make their way up Cathedral Street. Many cross themselves as the statue passes; some even kneel and bow their heads. The pantomime adds to the reverence of the morning. Amalia's fado—the songs thought to have been born from gypsy prostitutes—is respectfully silenced by Mateus as she passes. Mateus makes the sign of the cross. Manuel can't cross himself. Behind the statue is the white top of the baldachin, sheltering the honored guests and priests from the sun. Four young altar boys struggle to hold its poles. They look concerned, afraid the wind will tear the canopy from their grip. Their faces betray their fear of failing. Manuel was an altar boy once and understands. He catches a glimpse of the men shaded underneath, and in an instant that same fear that he felt as a child courses through him once again.

"Who is that, Mateus?"

Mateus, still leaning out the window with his arms crossed on the sill, forces Manuel back into the room. "Stay inside, Manuel. Get away from the window." But Manuel resists and pushes his chest hard against Mateus's hand. "That's Commander Alberto Sousa of the *Gil Eannes.*" Mateus whispers through clenched teeth as if someone is listening. Manuel has never seen the commander. The commander's eyes trace Manuel's round face, take note of his blue eyes, and recognize the blond hair of the one they had called *Boneco,* the doll. Manuel Antonio Rebelo—found. It is then that Manuel thinks of the photographs and documentation that must have been splayed across the commander's desk only a few months earlier. It would have been his responsibility to explain the loss of one of his men, and it certainly would have been his troublesome duty to travel to Manuel's small town of Lomba da Maia and place a standard pewter cross in the hands of his mother. Manuel notes the commander's excitement, glimpses his eyes darting about, looking for a gracious way out of the procession. But he is cordoned off by the thick rope of people that line the road, carried away and redirected by the wave of men.

"You're not safe here any longer, Manuel. The commander could report you, have you deported."

"Not him, Mateus." With open palms Manuel presses Mateus's cheeks hard and directs his view again. "The priest, for Christ's sake. What is his name?" Manuel knows Mateus does not understand the desperation in his voice. He lets go of his friend's smoothly shaved cheeks; the white imprint of his trembling hands remains.

"Padre Carlos, Manuel. He's the parish priest at the basilica. If you would only come . . . Why?"

It isn't the priest's oversized horn-rimmed glasses that force Manuel's memory, but the way his body favors his left side.

Padre Carlos would ask him to stay later than the other altar boys. When everything had been stored in the rectory and turned quiet, he would lock the door and demand that Manuel kneel at the upholstered prayer bench; kneel down and pray to Our Lady who looked at them both atop her wooden shelf.

"Pray with conviction! Close your eyes," he'd whisper before reaching over Manuel's shoulder and placing his glasses at the base of *Nossa Senhora*'s bare feet, her chipped toes magnified through them. But Manuel couldn't. He wanted her to move her eyes. He wanted her to see. He wanted to reach up, take hold of the priest's glasses, and perch them on her thin nose. Then he wanted her to weep, flood the rectory until they were both submerged in a lake of salted tears. Manuel thought he could hold his breath, grasp his trusted grouper Big Lips' dorsal fin, and surge through the waves and out the church door. Padre Carlos would be caught in the swirl and drown. She never wept. The room remained dry. Padre Carlos was still there, standing behind him, close enough that Manuel could feel the heat of him. Manuel kept his sweaty palms close together, elbows placed on the soft pad. He wouldn't look back when Padre Carlos's breathing became deep and rhythmic, when he moaned;

he just squished his hands and fingers together even
harder until his nails surged to a paler shade of white.
Manuel would gaze up at *Nossa Senhora* and imagine Big
Lips swimming in the air, circling her head before disappearing. The moaning would fade just before the obligatory five "Our Father"s. Padre Carlos would reach over
Manuel's shoulder and offer his trembling hand and gar-
net ring to kiss. "Those who serve me, serve God."

Manuel would run home, struggle to catch his breath
along the uneven road. "It's all right—he's not hurting
me," he'd repeat to himself. Once home he would move
to his room with an inconspicuous gait and lock the
door. Big Lips would pop out of his head. The gentle
giant would open and close his balloon-like mouth, fanning him with his transparent fins. It lasted three years
and Manuel's mother never knew.

> . . . *Listen to me well*
> *you Promised Land,*
> *if you love me*
> *I will be your most faithful slave.*
> *I will turn from my past*
> *to jump in your fire.*
> *I bear the map of the dreams*
> *I lost . . .*

They revel in the noise against the evening sky. The moon
lights the sails of the moored White Fleet, proud soldiers
in the still harbor. Mateus says it isn't safe in St. John's.
He tells Manuel the commander and his men are prob-
ing. Manuel had been the first man the commander lost

at sea. Mateus says the commander never believed he
had drowned; thinks it was all a ruse to escape Portugal
and his military obligation. He will not allow any sub-
terfuge to take seed, germinate in the hearts and minds
of those he has been charged with. Mateus assures
Manuel that if found, the commander will most certainly
force his return.

Head down, Manuel follows the remains of the once
glorious carpet of petals. It is now nothing more than a
crushed layer of confetti. The lines of the path are
blurred to the many who dance and drink. Others curl up
in doorways to sleep, while in one archway he steps near
the steady hum that emanates from a straddling pair. It is
a carnival. The *fadistas* weave in and out of homes, bal-
conies, and bars, singing their sorry attempts in falsetto.
Some try to duel in fado before erupting in laughter. But
it is the faithful ones with the candles, holding their small
flames of hope as they crawl up the street on their blood-
ied knees, who guide Manuel, under the gates and up to
the large oak doors that guard those within.

It is midnight and the thick walls of the Basilica of St.
John the Baptist dull the noise outside. It is gloomy inside.
He chooses to sit underneath a painting of Salome offering King Herod John the Baptist's head on a platter. Small
pools of light are cast from the ascending rows of prayer
votives that have been pushed against the wall. There are
people here, kneeling and praying, breathing in the smell
of melting wax, lemon wood polish, and stale mums.
Unlike Manuel, they are not waiting for the priest.

When Manuel was eight, he was summoned by Padre
Carlos one last time. The priest stood in front of the

altar as Manuel walked up to him. He reached into the money basket set on the altar. He offered a coin. When Manuel didn't take it, he reached for Manuel's balled fist and tried to peel his fingers open. He held Manuel's hand tight. He slipped the coin into Manuel's pocket. He was about to say something but Manuel wouldn't let him. Manuel turned before the priest uttered any words and walked back up the aisle. He reached into his pocket and pulled out the lint-covered coin, dropped it into the holy water at the church entrance, and wiped his hand across his pants. Manuel remembers hearing the sound of the coin hitting the crystal bottom before he punched open the heavy wooden doors, pushed his way out onto the worn steps of the church, into the warm air.

An hour has passed. Manuel's eyes move from the ornate relief that glorifies the ceiling to *Nossa Senhora de Fátima*'s blank expression in the dim light. The candles lit at her feet cast shadows that slash her features, elongate her nose, and bring one brow to a point.

"*Nossa Senhora,* please show me what is right." He is surprised by his own whisper.

He waits, but nothing. The church is warm. He turns to leave. Mateus said he would mail his letters. The boat leaves at one in the morning and then onto a train that will take him to a place many of *them* go, Montreal or Toronto. Mateus has written it all down. Manuel is about to cross himself, bends his knee slightly to genuflect, but then turns to walk down the aisle.

"Bless you, my son." His cassock flicks Manuel's shin as the black shape whirs by him.

"Padre Carlos!"

He turns. He is small. Not how Manuel remembers him.

"What is it, *filho*?"

"I'm not your son."

Padre Carlos tilts his head in distant recognition; he's trying to place the young man before him.

"I'm Manuel . . . Manuel Rebelo of Lomba da Maia." His eyes widen. "You used to say, 'Those who serve me . . . serve God.'"

Manuel's fists are hard, his knuckles white. The restraint in his voice is slipping away. Although Padre Carlos is his focus, he can see a flurry of people getting up from the pews, shifting away from them. Manuel surges toward the old priest. Bewildered, Padre Carlos shrivels and moves back. He raises his ringed finger to his mouth. "Shhh," he sounds.

Manuel catches the sparkle of red and the pleading in the priest's face. He hears some squeals, cries of *"Policia! Meu deus, Policia!"*

"I was a boy!" he yells. The echo comes back to him three, four, five times.

Padre Carlos stumbles backward, moves like a scurrying crab. He hits the base that supports *Nossa Senhora de Fátima*. The flames flicker, she teeters. Crouched beneath her, he cowers and makes the sign of the cross. His glasses askew, Manuel sees the whites of his eyes. He came to hurt him but the priest is so small. In a remarkable instant the anger and grief of his past leave him, only to be replaced by his fado, and the burning flame, which once had warmed him when he thought of home, is extinguished.

Manuel turns to leave then looks back. To steady himself, raise himself from the floor, Padre Carlos grabs on to the posts that provide temporary footing for the statue. She leans dangerously, rocks to right herself again, and then falls onto the base. There are cries of horror and wails of disbelief. Her head comes off cleanly and rolls down the aisle, chasing Manuel. He stops it under his foot. Her crown is flattened on one side. Her eyes stare at Manuel but they do not see. Maybe she will cry now . . .

> *Say good-bye to the sea, say good-bye*
> *Though the heavens may open*
> *And smile onto the place I was born,*
> *filled with the things I know.*
> *I will not come back from the sea.*
> *Do not weep, do not cry—*
> *only sing for my dream and . . .*
> *pray for me.*

~ MADE OF ME ~

IT WAS HER TURN TO GO. They all sat in Manuel's living room. His sister kept staring at the money that would pay for her flight piled on the coffee table. She alone sobbed in the silent room. Georgina brushed past Manuel and his brother Jose to sit beside her sister-in-law Candida.

"It will be okay, Candida. *Acalmar.* Shhhhh," Georgina whispered as she dabbed a tissue across Candida's upper lip and with her other hand caressed her back in large circles.

"But I don't want to go. I've made a life for myself here, far away from her hateful voice."

Her brothers sat on the crushed-velvet couch with their heads between their knees, staring at the carpet. Jose got up and left the room.

"Manuel, please—you didn't see the way she left me." She clutched her older brother's sleeve, twisted his cuff and the hair on his forearm. Manuel did not wince, just remained fixed, his expression betraying nothing. Georgina urged Manuel with her not-so-subtle facial expressions—to soothe, to console. Nothing.

"You were here—you didn't see." Candida choked on her words, wiped her nose with her sleeve. Manuel dragged his fingers across his son's jumble of blond hair. In silence, he offered the boy his hand and they left the women alone in the room.

Manuel passed by his brother Jose, who sat at the kitchen dinette drinking a beer. Manuel moved to the sink and smiled as he helped Antonio to sit atop the counter. Manuel knew his son—the boy he had named after the father he himself barely knew—would need his guidance to grow into a proper man, the kind of man that would thrive in this land he had made his home.

Manuel raised a bottle of Molson's Export Ale to his lips. The blue ship with all those sails on the label always reminded him of the place his family came from, of the Portuguese with their proud tradition of shipbuilding and exploration. "Jose, what *exactly*—" Manuel stopped, not because he didn't know what to ask but because he was afraid the question would lead him to a place he was quite content to leave alone. "What happened to Candida? You were there, you saw it."

"*Estupida.* She was so stupid, that girl, sometimes," Jose said.

Jose recounted the story, how Candida had found a used lipstick under a church pew, how she always had ideas of being a movie star, the kind that filled the smoky screens, always doing her hair in crimped waves when their mother just wanted her to get the house in order, to wash the dishes or sweep.

"It happened shortly after you left; soon after we thought you were . . . dead, at sea. *Mãe* was distraught and . . ."

Manuel looked over at his six-year-old son to see if the words his brother had spoken had entered the boy's head. He thought for an instant that it might be best to ask his son to leave, but chose not to. It was important to know things; knowledge was a kind of protection. Parents had an obligation to teach, he thought. Antonio just sat on the counter, prodding the dead fish in the sink with a straw.

"Candida was so caught up in her silly fantasy that, I guess, she lost track of all time, ran home, and forgot to wipe her lips clean. She sat at the dinner table and smiled, her lips as dark as black cherries."

Manuel scraped his knife quickly against the scales of the fish, sparkles flicking into the air. He smiled at Antonio's joy as the boy picked some scales from Manuel's stubble and hair. Antonio's gentleness aroused a fervent love for his son. But, it also frightened Manuel; his son was too meek, too full of his mother's milk to live out his promise. Manuel pointed the tip of the knife into the white belly of the fish, punctured it, and slit the fish up to the gills to clean its insides. Antonio grimaced, tucked his chin into his shoulder every time Manuel's fingers dug in and tore out the innards.

Jose continued his story—how Maria Theresa da Conceição Rebelo had stood behind her daughter Candida and stroked her hair, hummed a song she was fond of singing to them when they were small, before their father died. But then the humming faded, her fingers curled and tangled themselves in Candida's hair. She lifted her off the chair by her hair, and smeared the red lipstick across her chin and up to her ears. "'*Puta! Eu não quero putas nesta casa.*'" Candida's eyes were wide like a frightened horse s; she was snorting, trying to breathe through her mother's strong hands. "Remember those hands, Manuel?"

Manuel looked at his own hands, his strong fists covered in blood. He slammed the fish and knife into the sink. His brother turned his beer bottle, quarter turns, tearing at the label, the blue *navio*.

"And there she lay, beaten and alone on the dirt road, thrown out for a harlot at sixteen."

"Doesn't that hurt?" Antonio whispered.

"No." He offered his son the next fish and tried to place the knife in his hand. "Fish have little brains, *filho*, so small they can't even feel."

"Your hands, I mean." Antonio's soft eyes looked up at his father. Manuel did not respond. His son's stare had moved to the blood-soaked tea towel. Some of the fish were still twitching, their red gills fanning on the sides of their heads.

"They want their guts back," Antonio mumbled. He jumped down from the counter and ran down the hall.

~

That summer they gathered for her funeral—even though she wasn't dead yet. The phone call had traveled under the deep green Atlantic, sped along countless wires and nodes before it tumbled into 55 Palmerston Avenue with a crackled, "Manuel?"

"Yello," Manuel answered in his most proper tone.

"Manuel, is that you? Can you hear me? She says she wants to see you before she dies."

Manuel placed the receiver against his chest to muffle the staticky voice. He had been dreading this call.

"Manuel, please come. She's not ready. She's close but—"

Candida had only been there a week when she called. Within days, Manuel had secured the tickets. He had intended for his brother Jose and his sister Albina to return with him, but couldn't afford the fares. He had pleaded with the travel agent to allow his children to sit on their laps, freeing two seats. The agent continued to process the passports as if his request was ridiculous.

He had come home and moved behind Georgina as she washed the dishes. He fanned the tickets in front of her face, then placed them on the counter next to the sink. Georgina said nothing. She continued to wash, her hands searching in the water. She didn't bother to rinse the dishes, just placed the suds-covered plates to dry on the rack and moved to their bedroom. Manuel followed. Not once did she look at him as she pulled her slip and skirts from the chest of drawers and whipped them on top of the bed. Words could not bridge the hesitation in Manuel and the awkward fear his wife had of returning. He had reassured her that they would never go back. But Manuel had convinced himself that this might be the opportunity to show everyone, especially his mother, that everything he had sacrificed to make a life for himself in Canada had been worth it.

Manuel sat beside Antonio on the plane, watched with pride as his son looked out the small window, convinced that the white flecks in the ocean were migrating whales shooting water through their blowholes or, even better, sharks.

"They're not sharks, stupid," Terezinha said. She was ten, and still upset that her mother had allowed her to bring only Thumbelina and not her Easy-Bake oven. *Oh,* filha, *it's too big,* hadn't been a good enough answer. Terezinha had stomped her feet and hadn't stopped sulking since. Manuel placed a hand on her head and turned it to face forward as he pushed her down into her seat. He loved both his children but he saw his daughter's spirit as a bent nail, something that needed to be hammered straight before it could be used. His wife shared the same concern but reassured Manuel that it was a kind of moxie that would serve her well; manners and etiquette didn't necessarily get girls very far. In Canada, women could show their strength and independence and even be rewarded in life.

The road to the village—there was still only one—snaked its way along the coast, hugging the cliffs so closely that if Manuel held his arm out the window he could scrape his fingertips across the damp rock wall. Large balls of pink and blue hydrangeas lined the road like weeds. Manuel remembered going out early in the morning during the *Festa de Nossa Senhora do Rosário,* his town's patron saint, to cull their large heads and pluck their flake-like petals into linen potato sacks. The streets needed to be decorated.

Manuel smiled when every so often the children were startled by the sudden pounding on the roof of the taxi—the gush of natural spring water falling from fissures in the rock above. He watched as Antonio pressed his face into a red balloon and squished it against the car window to make the world outside turn pink. Manuel couldn't drag his eyes away from his son as he practiced the few Portuguese phrases he had been taught—*bom dia, obrigado,* and *olá!*—repeated them over and over into the balloon. The droning sound made Manuel's ears itch and he was reminded of his own anxiety.

As if sensing Manuel's irritation, Antonio, dressed in his new blue suit, moved to his mother's lap and rode her knee's nervous bounce. Manuel knew that his mother, if she was still well enough, would see her grandson and recognize his greatness. He looked at Terezinha, a cotton ball in her First Communion dress. Just before leaving, her mother had cut her fine hair short, trimmed neatly around the lip of a bowl. Manuel had been angry but his wife had responded, "She's my daughter, she needed a haircut." Terezinha sat up front with the taxi driver. She wasn't afraid of anyone or anything. Every once in a while Georgina would reach over the seat to tug at Terezinha's ear when she was asking the driver too many questions.

Georgina wasn't the one his mother would have chosen for her son. Before the wedding, blood had been shed and hateful words exchanged, words that even

Manuel had never dared to ask about. Manuel knew when it was best to stand back and leave things alone.

"Okay?" Manuel asked.

Georgina didn't answer for a while. Only when he turned away did she respond. "She better not bring up the past. Or else—"

Manuel reached over and folded her hand into his.

He felt like a boy again as he gulped in the air that rushed past his face through the open window. Antonio mimicked his father by sticking his face out the window, but his mother pulled him back in by the scruff of his neck, careful not to crumple the crease in his collar, and tried to straighten his unruly hair. Every so often Terezinha would turn around and roll her eyes; she couldn't sit still and began to tap her doll's head rhythmically against the window. Manuel tried to reach over and hold her in place. She wriggled for a while. Manuel knew that the rolling green hills against the azure sea held nothing for his daughter; she wanted people with names—she had heard about them all and she wanted to see if they were as real in person.

Not much had changed in the past ten years. It struck Manuel that he had thought of Lomba da Maia as a town frozen in time, its people fixed and unchanged. Only now, upon his return, did he feel their lives were set in motion once again.

The taxi drove slowly past the steps leading up to the church, *Nossa Senhora do Rosário.* Manuel tried hard not to look at the worn steps that led to its large wooden doors. So much of his life had been affected by what had happened within the cold walls of that church. He tried to think of practical things, to get his mind away from his troubled thoughts. They rounded the corner onto a dirt road, the taxi windows now covered with a thin layer of dust that swarmed around the car. There were the same small houses in bright white. Some old women leaned out of their windows with rosaries dangling from their gnarled fists. Manuel felt compelled to fight his recognition of these people. He saw angry dogs, tied up with string, that barked and flung themselves into the air, only to be yanked back, their bodies twisted as they tumbled onto the dirt road. Sweat moistened the new suit Manuel had bought at Eaton's. As the taxi passed, some men stopped pushing their wooden carts to straighten up and slightly lift their straw hats. Antonio shuffled back onto his father's lap and Manuel anticipated his son's question.

"The children are working in the fields. You'll see them soon enough."

Antonio smiled and slumped back into Manuel's chest.

Manuel reached for his handkerchief, dabbed some spit on it and wiped the chocolatey corners of Antonio's mouth, cleaned the corners of his blue eyes. He then parted his hair, smoothed both sides with his unsteady hands. He cupped his son's ears and cheeks and tilted his face back—forced Antonio to look at him.

"Don't be afraid, be strong," he whispered.

The car stopped at the end of a road. Terezinha was the first to step out and unruffle her dress. She squatted quickly to wipe her patent-leather shoes with an open palm. She was followed by Georgina, who knew better and grabbed her daughter's hand before she could race up the steps into a house she had never seen. Manuel saw that holding on to the girl was the only thing calming his wife's nerves. Antonio stepped out before Manuel. They stood and faced the little white house with the same worn indigo blue door and matching windows that Manuel remembered. He turned to look at the houses across the road, the same dried-up well and the expanse of field that disappeared over a cliff into the sea. His trance was broken by Terezinha. She tucked Thumbelina into an armpit, grabbed his hand, and tugged him toward the people waiting at the front door. Georgina shook her head the way she always did when Terezinha's boldness took hold of everyone. Surprised at himself, Manuel allowed the tears to roll down his cheeks.

A cluster of familiar faces had gathered near the front door. Manuel noticed that they too were dressed in their Sunday finery; the men wore shoes and shirts with sleeves that covered their sun-browned arms and the women wore dresses with floral patterns undisturbed by aprons or housecoats. Their hair was pinned back, away from their ruddy faces.

Manuel's abrupt beginning in Canada had made it possible to dismiss a difficult past. But for a moment, he admitted to himself that his recollections of life in the Azores, on the tiny island of São Miguel, in the backward village of Lomba da Maia, had been distorted in some way by his failure to fulfill the promise he had set for himself. As quickly as the gloomy thought had entered his mind, it left him.

Manuel smiled and nodded as his family engulfed him in hugs and hearty sobs hailing his return. They moved toward Georgina, who smiled awkwardly at their uncertain shows of affection. Manuel could see Antonio giving in to the fawning women and Terezinha pushing them away as they giggled at the young girl's incredulity. They made way for the prodigal son, steering him through the house with their close-mouthed smiles and approving nods. They had moved from the morning brightness into the dark cool of his mother's house.

Manuel paused at the doorway to his mother's bedroom. He heard the sounds of insects and the dried cornstalks rustling in the light breeze as he lowered his chin in prayer before slowly opening the door.

A yellow afterglow stained the lace curtains and filtered into the dusty gloom of the room. She just lay there. Not the strong, towering presence he remembered. She wore a simple black dress. White wisps peeked through her black veil. Candida sat precariously on the bed's edge. The show of relief was evident. Manuel moved toward her, reaching back to bring his two children in front of him. Antonio shuffled behind his sister and peered through the crook of her arm. Terezinha took a step forward without any urging. She held her Thumbelina doll in front of her grandmother's face and pulled the string on the doll's back. There was restrained laughter as the doll's head spun around and around until the string grew shorter and disappeared.

"*Terezinha, Mãe. Tua neta,*" Manuel whispered.

She held up the doll again and was about to tug at the string when Manuel's mother slowly raised her arm to stop her.

Manuel saw how his mother's eyes moved to his wife, who stood by his side.

"*Atrevida—é morena como a tua mãe.*"

Georgina moved toward her mother-in-law. She wouldn't allow this woman to call her daughter bold and dark-skinned. She yanked Terezinha backward to her side, leaving Antonio exposed.

Candida looked ragged. She was resentful of the duty that had fallen on her, and she carelessly dragged a cloth along her mother's forehead. Manuel noticed how Candida teetered on the bed, as if still afraid she could be hurt by the woman who lay helplessly beside her. Candida invited Antonio to come closer with her toothy, crooked smile. He took a step forward only when Manuel pressed on his neck, urging the boy to move in his grandmother's direction. Antonio took another hesitant step, looked up at the red balloon floating over his head, its thin ribbon tied securely to his wrist.

"*Antonio, vem ver a tua avó*—go see—go see her."

Manuel had moved forward with his son until they both stood close to the old woman's bed. Manuel took in the smell of damp mingled with mothballs that floated from her linens. These were not the smells he associated with his mother; he remembered her smell of bleach, always the sterility of bleach. He looked at her face. It was shiny, slippery like the skin of a freshly caught fish. Sweat moved into the creases and wrinkles of her face, rivulets ran down from the corners of her eyes, her forehead, down her cheeks where they would certainly pool behind her head.

"*Mãe, o meu filho, Antonio.*" Manuel became very aware that he was presenting his son as if an offering. He felt a quick tug on his sleeve, a reprimand from his wife.

Seeing his helpless mother settled Manuel's past.
There was no need to hold on to things that had weighed
so heavily on him, that had become obstacles, or so he
rationalized, to all the things he had wanted from life.
Manuel urged Antonio to kiss her, hoping to show everyone that he had raised his boy to respect his elders. The
boy puckered up and leaned his head in his grandmother's direction, into the smell of sickness. Her face
turned to meet his. Her flaking lips parted, showing her
dark, gummed mouth. Her lips reached out for her
grandson. She looked at Antonio and lit up before she
lay back on her pillow. *Relief.* Though her eyes were shut,
Manuel could see the faint outline of her irises through
her translucent eyelids.

"*Naõ és rei . . . tu és mais de que rei,*" she muttered softly.

Manuel's chest puffed. He looked at Georgina's
flushed face and then scanned the adoring smiles around
the room. They all began to clap the same way the
Portuguese clapped when their plane landed safely. *You
are not a king . . . you are more than a king;* it was his mother's
pronouncement—her blessing. Manuel brushed past his
son and fell heavily to his knees beside his mother's bed.
He reached for her spotted hands and brought them to
his lips. His sobs mixed with the sobs of others as the
room spun in its stifling summer heat.

She seemed weightless as he moved her across the room
toward Candida, who stood waiting behind one of the
caned kitchen chairs. Manuel sat her down as Candida
pressed her bosom firmly against the back of her mother's

head and held her shoulders against the chair. Candida
laughed and hummed "O Christmas Tree" as Manuel
wove a rope around his mother as if trimming her with a
string of colored lights. Manuel shot Candida a look of
reproach. Candida then took over with her collection of
ruined pantyhose and tied her mother to the chair in the
areas that required more flexibility: wrists and collar-
bone. She then covered their handiwork with a black,
knitted shawl.

"Don't worry, *Mãe*, we're not about to let you miss
mass," Manuel said.

Candida struggled with her mother's shoes.

"She'd die if she missed Sunday mass."

"Candida!"

Manuel looked to the doorway where both his children stood. Terezinha seemed amused by what she had
just witnessed.

"She's going to die," she said.

Antonio swatted his sister away like a fly.

"And when she does . . . I'm going to dance on her
grave." Manuel moved toward his daughter, who ran
down the hallway. "Everyone will dance. I know they
will. I heard them—" she continued to yell.

Manuel was intercepted by his cousins who came
into the house, respectfully clean. They were dressed in
suits that were far too large or uncomfortably snug. They
greeted him, smiled at his panting daughter who stood
behind her mother in the kitchen, then moved into the
bedroom where each grabbed a leg of the chair. On
Manuel's count they hoisted his mother into the air.
Terezinha giggled when she saw her grandmother's head

jerk and fall onto her right shoulder. Manuel saw his son trying hard not to laugh. He looked to his wife, who responded by giving both children a disapproving pinch. The men lowered themselves through the doorway and out into the already warm morning just as the bells began to peal. They turned themselves toward the church and like soldiers they began to march. Everyone took their places behind Maria Theresa da Conceição Rebelo, strapped into her chair, floating. They walked up the unpaved road. The neighbors, who stood on their front porches or were on their way to church themselves, bowed their heads. Even in her weakened state, Manuel's mother, with eyelids barely open, was still respected and feared in town.

"Your grandmother wants to see you," Manuel said. He had untangled his mother and already placed her back in bed. He found his children in their bedroom changing out of their Sunday clothes.

"I'll tell her the story of Hansel and Gretel," Terezinha offered.

"Only Antonio." It hurt Manuel to say it, to make his daughter feel that she wasn't important, that she didn't count. It was the same thing his mother had been fond of doing to his own siblings, always choosing him over the others. Manuel was reluctant at first to give in to his mother's demand but then acquiesced, knowing she did not have much time.

Terezinha ran out of the room and headed for the women who were in the backyard chasing the hens for

Sunday dinner. Manuel looked at his son. It was a difficult thing to ask of the boy, who twirled the ribbon of his balloon between his fingers. He didn't look up to meet his father's pleading face.

"Would you like me to come in with you?" he offered.

Antonio said nothing but moved into his father's outstretched arms and blotted his tears on his father's shoulder. Manuel rubbed his son's back.

He moved out into the hallway carrying Antonio in his arms. He could see Terezinha through the back door snuffing her face into her mother's belly as she tried to wrap her mother's apron over her head in shame. Georgina stroked her daughter's head.

"*Vamos, filho,*" he urged, "nothing is going to happen to you." And as if to put his son's mind at ease, "I'll leave the door wide open. I'll stay with you, okay? . . . Okay."

The shutters were closed. The only natural light burst from between the shutters' slats like beams. A candle on her nightstand lit statues of saints and some black-and-white unframed pictures that leaned against an old clock. Manuel sat down on the wooden stool beside her bed and lifted Antonio to sit on his knee.

"Can she see me, *Pai*?"

As if in answer, her arm came out from under the covers and slowly shook through the air. Manuel saw how his son's eyes followed her hand in fear until her yellow nail clicked against a sepia picture of a young man.

"*Avô,*" she whispered.

"Your grandfather," Manuel translated.

Manuel looked at the picture of his father and then

at one of himself that also sat on her nightstand; the resemblance was strong. She pointed to a picture of Antonio standing with a fishing rod and a small sunfish he had caught. The picture had been taken in High Park. Manuel remembered sending it to his mother along with a twenty-dollar bill; unbeknownst to his wife, he would send money when he could.

"*Você veio de mim*," she whispered. Antonio turned to his father to make sense of the words.

"You are made of me," Manuel whispered.

She smiled for a while, nodding her head, but then her smile vanished. The candle flickered. Georgina had entered the room silently.

"*Nunca . . . nunca . . .*" she repeated as she gently lifted her son out of Manuel's lap and pulled him behind her, out of her mother-in-law's view. Georgina leaned over to the dying woman's ear and whispered between gritted teeth, "*Nunca* . . . there is no evil in this child. He's mine and you will not destroy him, not him too."

Manuel would not interfere; she had every right to be angry with the woman who had made her life so painful and difficult. She tugged at Antonio and they moved across the room. She slammed the door behind her, leaving Manuel alone with his mother.

"My children are *my* blood and flesh, *Mãe*."

The old woman looked lonely with her pride. It was her partiality for Manuel that forced him to remain.

Before the rooster could announce a new day, Manuel awoke to the high-pitched wails of a woman—yells of anguish and horror. He rushed into his mother's room to find her lying on the bedroom floor, unwilling to let anyone help her back to her deathbed.

"*Em nome do Pai e do Filho e do Espírito Santo,*" making the sign of the cross with jerking motions. "*Em nome do Pai e do Filho e do . . .*" She dug her heels into the floor and dragged her body up against a wall as she pointed in hysterics to a shriveled red balloon that had settled on top of her chamber pot. Candida, in a momentary fit of duty, lowered herself to the floor and rocked the old woman from behind, whispering unknown things into her mother's ear. Manuel stood helpless. The old woman turned to her son and then to her grandson, who stood rubbing his eyes. In horror she breathed out her final judgment, a gasp of odorous air exhaled, and sank into Candida's arms. The silence was shattered as Candida let go of her mother's limp body, allowed the woman's head to thump onto the wooden floor.

At first there was quiet, and then Candida's contained chuckle, which Manuel took for crying. But he soon realized his mistake. Manuel scanned his family as they sleepily gathered in his mother's bedroom.

"Candida, have you no respect? Control yourself. Our mother is dead."

"Oh Manuel, I just couldn't . . ."

She tried to compose herself as she sat hugging her knees beside the lifeless body, occasionally touching their mother's cooling forehead with her big toe—just to make sure.

"After all these years—" She caught hold of herself. "All she said was, 'I'm dying. My stomach . . . all gone . . .

torn out of me . . . gone.'" She pointed to the balloon on the chamber pot, rolled onto her side, and laughed into the plank floor.

The hem of the old woman's nightdress cut across her upper thighs, her scrawny legs tangled and melded like a slippery tail. Antonio dragged a blanket off the bed, pulled it over his grandmother's legs, careful not to cover her face. Manuel took a step toward his sister but was held back by his wife.

"Leave her be. She has her reasons," Georgina said.

That morning, no one would return to the warmth of their beds. The women were left to prepare the body for a short wake and then burial. It was going to be another hot day, there were things to be done.

"She was a remarkable woman, my mother."

Manuel sat in the kitchen with his cousins. He had roused them from their sleep, called on them to gather at his mother's home even though the sun had not risen yet.

"You've been away too long, Manuel," Augusto said. "Time has healed, or it's made you forget."

"I haven't forgotten. But there were crops to sow, animals to tend, an ocean floor to harvest. I remember her storming into class that day—'Senhora Oliveira,' she said, 'school is getting in the way of filling their bellies,' and we left."

The men began to smile, their memories stoked by this simple recollection.

"Remember, Manuel, leaving before the sun rose to plunge into the frigid waters to catch octopus, eel, and red snapper? Sometimes you would waste the day lying in the sun, rolling in the warm black sand. Remember?"

"I remember," Manuel said. "She would lock the door if we came home with nothing." Manuel knew that the door was always open for him; it was only Jose who was denied his warm bed. "My brother Jose and I would huddle together in the barn until the morning, when we would return to the sea once again to dive for food."

They kept on drinking. Georgina was now in the kitchen plucking some chickens by the sink, and every so often flailing at the cigarette smoke that hung in the room. Over the course of the morning their words had begun to slow down, get longer. Manuel spoke of his sister Albina, who made sure the sheets and clothing were laundered and mended; they were poor but his mother refused to have her children dirty. He moved to Jose, who tended the six cows, two pigs, and dozen or so hens. Then there was Mariano, the shifty-eyed one, as he was known by the neighbors, who seeded the land and harvested the crops. And as if on cue, Candida walked in as Manuel recalled how his little sister was supposed to be the gatherer of fruit and berries but dreamed of becoming a movie star and making it big.

Candida began rattling the pots louder and then slammed a cast iron frying pan on top of the stove. They all turned toward her but it wasn't enough to stop Manuel. He was now drunk and his words became tempered with bitterness.

"She was so proud of her well-oiled machine. But it was all based on fear!" He shouted these words down the hallway.

Terezinha stood there, bathing in the silence that followed her father's outburst. He saw his daughter take hold of a dead chicken that lay on the kitchen counter. She clasped the headless animal by its feet. Terezinha bit her lips as she swung the chicken and tried to spell her name on the kitchen floor with droplets of blood.

Manuel then looked at Antonio, still in his pajamas; he sat cross-legged in the corner winding his wrist with the thin ribbon that had once held on to his balloon. So gentle, so empty of the spirit Manuel had wanted the boy to possess.

Manuel stood outside his mother's bedroom looking through the half-opened door. It wasn't his place. They washed her pale body by candlelight. Smoke and the smell of beeswax filled the room and wafted into the hall where he stood. Manuel could see Georgina through the haze, passing a cloth along his mother's neck, pulling the dead woman's frail arm out to the side as she washed the white skin on the inside of her wrist, elbow. Candida, resolved to her final duty, gathered the burial dress in her fists, like a sock just before it's pulled over one's foot. She placed the opening over her mother's head, struggled and fought to pull it down her already stiffening body. Candida then reached for a neatly folded parcel of tissue paper. She carefully unpacked a tortoiseshell comb with scalloped edges, a gift from Manuel that had never been worn. She looked at Manuel before plunging it into the side of her mother's hair. Georgina covered the woman's head with the traditional burial wimple as Terezinha, who had been standing by the shutters, came over and smiled at her father as she helped to fluff her grandmother's dress. Georgina caught him looking and raised her hand to ward him off, to leave the women to their job. He stood fixed. They garnished her with branches of pine and cedar, tucking them under her, framing her. His mother's knobby fingers were forced together across her stomach and her beaded rosary woven between her stiffening hands.

Manuel felt Antonio lean against his leg.

"The cedar helps cover up the smell of death," he told his son. He raised him up, kissed him on the neck and lost himself in his son's familiar sweet smell, away from the putrification that wafted from the contained room.

As the moon sank into the ocean, the day began to fill with villagers lining up outside to pay their respect. Some wanted to see it for themselves—*could she really be dead?* Others just wanted to touch her—*a saint,* some said.

Manuel wasn't sure of their names. The women were shrouded in veils and the men wore no hats, their hair parted and wet. People knelt by the dead woman's bed and whispered prayers. Some were brave enough to bend over and kiss her pallid forehead or adjust her clothing, a collar or sleeve. Some even cried, interrupting the steady hum of communal vespers.

There is comfort in death, Manuel thought, *the freedom to behave in a way that could not have been possible if someone were alive.*

They would then make their way around the room, offering the family their prayers and whispered things. Manuel saw how the women would cup Antonio's face in their rough hands and prick his cheek with their lips. Terezinha held on to Thumbelina, repeatedly tugging at the string in hopes of reviving the doll's head. Some of the women tried to kiss her cheek but most just tapped her head in recognition.

Manuel could hear Padre Alberto begin to recite the rosary outside his mother's window. He could hear the shuffling crowd that had gathered and repeated the words of the priest in unison. The final mourners trickled out of their front doors to gather quietly on the dirt road in front of the house, to wait for the family, to pray and offer her a final mass, to process and bury her. It had to be done within the day—the town still wasn't large enough to make a funeral home a viable business—and so the town had no choice but to adhere to tradition. Anyway, it was best for the departed to enter the Kingdom of Heaven the old-fashioned way—right away.

Candida pulled back the sheets to reveal her mother fully dressed in black like an ominous cloud.

Georgina held on to the woman's thin ankles, and Candida—only after much urging—tucked her arms under her mother's shoulders. On the count of three they lifted her stiff body and awkwardly dropped her into the pine coffin. Manuel caught his children's awe as their grandmother floated straight and hard as a tabletop. Georgina arranged the dead woman neatly and properly in the box lined with raw linen, then took it upon herself to lower the lid.

Terezinha held on to her mother's gloved hand as she drew aside the lace curtains, flung the shutters open to lean out the window. She signaled for the priest to begin the funeral march that would take them to *Nossa Senhor do Rosário* for the last time. They were just about to begin when Manuel motioned the pallbearers to stay where they were, to give them all a few moments alone as a family.

"Come here, Candida," Manuel said. Georgina closed the shutters.

Manuel pried open the lid and slipped something inside the coffin. Candida reluctantly moved close to the lip of the box. Manuel felt his children nudge their way between them and grasp onto the ridge of the casket. Georgina moved beside her sister-in-law.

"A cold fish. She was no mother to me," Candida heaved.

"She took so much from you, Candida. She took from me too, but no more," Georgina said.

Georgina reached for the photograph of her husband and her son that Manuel had placed inside, tucked somewhere in the ripples of fabric, and slipped it into her purse.

Candida reached inside her purse and pulled out a silver cylinder. She twisted it, then lowered her hand to her mother's white face. She smeared the woman's mouth with bright red lipstick, went beyond her lips and up toward her cheeks like a child who chose not to color inside the lines. She trembled as she hummed a song that Manuel faintly recalled. She took a step back, cocked her head as if to admire her work. She looked to her brother, who moved away from them until his back pressed against the cold wall. He understood as much as he could but was beginning to feel uncomfortable. Candida then rammed the tube between the dead woman's hands, where it lay next to the jet-bead rosary and silver crucifix.

She took one last look, smiled, and gently lowered the lid.

Everyone waited outside. The box was lifted onto the men's shoulders. They carried her with heads down, up the uneven road, kicking at the wild dogs with their now dusty shoes if they dared come near to sniff. As the procession wound its way up and passed *Nossa Senhora do Rosário*, Manuel noticed the sudden rustle of curtains, the occasional sign of the cross and the obligatory cries and sniffles from the men and women behind him. Terezinha walked in front of Manuel, holding on to her aunt's hand. Manuel drew his wife close to him. Antonio's arms were secured around his mother's neck. Manuel saw him pull his mother's veil over his head too. He whispered, "*Mãe*, how is she going to breathe? Why didn't they put some holes in the coffin?

"Fish need air to breathe too," Antonio said with conviction.

~ *BARNACLE LOVE* ~

MANUEL USED HIS FOREARMS to part the stalks of corn. His blood coursed through him. He forged ahead, swiping at the brittle stems, nursing the anger that had pressed on him ever since he had arrived back home and Silvia had said no.

Two weeks ago, with an eagerness that overcame jet lag and saw him abandon his luggage on the front stoop of his crumbling childhood home, he had dashed through the fields to meet with her. She had agreed to go to Canada in her letters, but it wasn't until he arrived, after some long anticipated and disappointing love-making, that she told him she didn't want to leave. Not prepared for her excuses, he had stormed through the cornfields, allowing the husks to thrash against his face. She was his intended, but his dream was his alone now. Her futile calls for him to return—"*Manuel! Volta,*

Manuel!"—receded as he broke through onto the dirt road.

A week passed. Silvia asked for a second meeting. He came into the clearing once again.

Silvia's eyes rested in the dark hollows of her face. She looked smaller now.

"I'll go! Is that what you want . . . I'll leave with you as your wife." She had crawled to him and tugged on his trousers with her chin up, pleading.

He grabbed her shoulders. "I don't want to begin my new life with a lie!"

She swiped the snot across her cheek. "But I've changed my mind. I'll make a life with you there if that's what you want." She reached for his hand and pulled him down as she arched her back. His knees buckled and she placed his hand between the warmth of her legs. She grasped his back to lower him even further.

He withdrew his hand and caressed her face. He whispered, "I thought it was what you wanted also," as he stood up to leave.

"Your mother said you would stay; that all I had to do was ask you to start a life with me here and that we would all be together. She said she knew you, she knew what you wanted and that everything would be okay." Silvia looked around now as if expecting someone or something to appear from within the thick crop of corn and save her. "She said it would all be okay."

He stormed up to Senhora Theresa's small house on Rua Nova. He walked straight up to the window, and with not even an inkling of restraint, he asked her for her daughter Georgina's hand.

~

Those who lived in the village of Lomba da Maia would often assemble in its cobbled square to hear Amalia's fados drifting out of Senhora Genevieve's gramophone and through her open window. Although she herself was deaf, the songs of lament served as a backdrop for the town square as the men smoked, balancing hand-rolled cigarettes on their cracked lips as they slammed their cards down, knuckles red on bistro tables. Their wives and women sat like aged schoolgirls, repeating their family histories, shared events borne from a past as if newly found. It was in that square, as a boy of six visiting for the first time, that Antonio heard the story of the blessed union between his mother and father.

Antonio sat in his shorts and navy blazer at the bottom of the steps that led up to the whitewashed church. His father, Manuel, who sat playing cards at the other end of the square, had insisted his wife and children be dressed to perfection. Terezinha sported a bowl cut that reminded Antonio of Casey from Mr. Dressup. She wore a simple dress and bobby socks. They both wore patent-leather shoes in the dusty heat of summer. Antonio sat with his legs opened in a V, playing with his marbles while his sister skipped around him and along the fancy loops and bordered patterns of inlaid black cobblestone.

"I can see your birdie, I can see your birdie, I can see . . ." Terezinha chimed, and pointed and snickered.

Antonio's reaction was immediate; he shut his legs and gathered the marbles that stuck to the back of his sweaty knees. He saw his father and took a few steps toward him but then saw the agitated look on his face. Antonio ran to his mother instead, who sat on a bench between her sister, Aunt Louisa, and her best friend, Carmen, whom she hadn't seen since she had left more than ten years ago. Aunt Candida had refused to stay after the funeral. She had departed on the first flight home.

They sat lazily licking their *gelados*. His mother dabbed beads of sweat from her face with her kerchief and raised the burden of her hair with her forearm to cool the back of her neck.

"What is it, *filho*?" she asked as Antonio crawled up and slipped into her lap. She offered him a lick of her *gelado*. Terezinha came running after Antonio but stopped behind the bench and took the weight of her mother's hair into her hands.

"Blow, *filha*."

His mother closed her eyelids in the refreshing pleasure of it all and raised her glistening face to the sun. She sunk further into the bench and Antonio enjoyed sliding down with her.

"Was it all worth it, Georgina?" Carmen asked.

"Carmen," she responded, "what my mother-in-law did will always remain with me. But, yes." She lifted Antonio's bangs with the side of her open palm. She looked at him through slit eyes and blew on his forehead through smiling lips. "I'd say it was all worth it."

Aunt Louisa turned to Carmen and whispered, "That woman's with the devil now." Georgina responded with a reproachful glance, as if to suggest the children had been through enough already, witnessed far more than they should have at their age. Antonio stopped twirling his mother's gold crucifix. Undeterred, Aunt Louisa began to tell the story of the wedding preparation . . .

Antonio could almost picture his mother's soft, plump arms and delicate fingers reaching up to the ceiling so that her mother and sister could shimmy the poof of white over her head. It was the town's wedding dress, the same one that all young girls in the village of Lomba da Maia wore when they married men they were barely allowed to know. They would wiggle their hips to allow the communal dress to sit as well as it could before it was unstitched, pinned, and stitched and seamed once again for that week's bride.

"Your father loved me," Grandmother Theresa had said to her daughter.

"Manuel loves me too."

"You are not the one he came for and—"

"And what, *Mãe*? Huh? Silvia was the one he came to Portugal for. Is that what you want to hear? Well, she said *no* . . . and I said yes."

Georgina knew very little about Manuel, other than that he was twenty-six and he looked forward to sharing a life in Canada. They weren't allowed to spend time together. She could only lean out the window as Manuel stood outside, his two feet planted firmly on the dirt road. That was just the way things were.

"That's the way they still are," Carmen added. The women laughed.

"I thought that what *was* there could grow." Georgina contemplated her words lazily. The women all nodded in agreement; Carmen even sighed.

Terezinha cupped her mouth with her hand to stop herself from giggling. All this talk of romance and marriage was too much for her. Luckily, Senhora Genevieve's small dog came yelping into the square, chasing after the hens. Terezinha saw it as a necessary diversion and ran after it—*tormenting things smaller than her is her specialty*, Antonio thought. Antonio stayed still, hopeful that his mother had forgotten he was sitting on her lap, breathing in her smell of Skin-So-Soft, she had purchased the whole line from the Avon catalogue.

Georgina said that Manuel's offer of marriage had been an ongoing topic of conversation for the better part of the week. It was his mother's duty to propose on his behalf, and she had done so grudgingly.

"'As you know, my son Manuel has chosen a different path,'" Aunt Louisa mocked. "I have heard, Maria," had been Grandmother Theresa's response. Grandmother Maria had held up her hand. This was something she *had* to do and it would be done as duty dictated.

"'He has now chosen your daughter.'" Aunt Louisa could still mimic the bitterness in her voice. "'One can only hope that your daughter is . . . a virgin.'"

The two women, Maria and Theresa, had been friends since childhood. Their words were few, but even back then Georgina had sensed they could read each other with an acuteness usually reserved for siblings.

"My mother was furious," Georgina said. "'That woman . . . she floats up to my front door in her black dress, saying, *You should be happy my Manuel has chosen your daughter.*'

"'Stop *Mãe*, please,' I had pleaded.

"'*One would hope she's a virgin, Theresa.* The nerve of that woman.'"

Grandmother Theresa had wiped the spittle from her lips, stepped back and sat on the wooden chair by the bedroom window. She had reached back, slid her black kerchief from her head and brought her graying hair up over her shoulder. She had begun to braid slowly as she gazed out the front window.

"'She doesn't want this to happen. She'll make it a hell for you.'

"'I'll be far away from her, *Mãe*, in Canada.'

"'She is a presence that will cross the oceans to Terra Nova. Mark my words. I know her. She has spoken of nothing else these last two years while her Manuel was away in Canada: Silvia, the heiress to forty head of cattle . . . *my Silvia, so* delicata, *will make him come home—will make a life for him here full of* fortuna. *I lost him once, I won't lose him again.'*

"I knelt before my mother and looked up at her fragile neck. 'I need to get away, *Mãe*. This is my chance.' I looked out my window toward the church of *Nossa Senhora do Rosário*. My mother continued braiding her hair and mumbling her prayers. Soon, she would knot the few strands that remained at the tip tightly to keep her braid in place. My hand rested on the windowsill and I'll always remember the heat of my mother's hand when she placed it over mine."

Antonio watched the dogs that lay carelessly in the middle of the road. Some had matted clumps or patches of fur peeling from their skin. Every so often, one would lift its head and lamely attempt to snap its crooked jowl at a fly before laying its head back down on the parched earth.

Antonio's mother looked down at him. She kissed his nose, drew him in close to her, then rested her chin on his head.

"I remember looking down the dusty street of Rua Nova until it disappeared into a wide swatch of blue. Beyond was my future."

Antonio rested the side of his head on his mother's chest. He could feel the crucifix digging into his temple as he looked across the square and met with his father's stern look. Antonio closed his eyes, pretended to sleep.

"Take this off, *filho*." Georgina seemed agitated by the heat and Antonio's drenched blazer. She fought to get him out of it. He slid down her bare legs and sat at her feet, just as Terezinha came bouncing along. She held her hands open, all plastered with white fur. Her worn Thumbelina was tucked under her arm. "*Mãe*, that stupid dog, Pocas or Pipocas or whatever, he was playing with my Thumbelina and look what he did!" Her doll's feet had been chewed off right up to the ankles, leaving her with hollow tubes for legs.

"She didn't work anymore, anyway," Antonio giggled.

His sister was about to pounce when she heard the sound of shuffling slippers and turned to see Senhora Genevieve coming toward them. She waved her hands and mouthed angry sounds that no one really understood. The women frowned and made pleading gestures that they were sorry. Senhora Genevieve grabbed Terezinha's hands and plucked at the white fur she had stripped from her dog's back. Georgina assured her that her daughter would be kept far away from her little dog. Senhora Genevieve was not satisfied as she turned and left. Terezinha stood behind her mother and picked what remained of the dog's fur, soft like candy floss, from between the webbing of her sweaty fingers.

It was obvious from Georgina's smile that she was fond of her daughter's resilience. Even at six, Antonio knew his mother saw something in his sister's spirit that reminded her of herself.

"To this day the village still speaks of your wedding, you know," Carmen offered.

"And to think it almost never happened," Georgina said.

"You had second thoughts?" Aunt Louisa sounded surprised.

Satisfied that she had roused interest, Georgina nodded. "I did, but I wouldn't let her win." She continued her story, spurred by the vision of Terezinha, who had kicked off her shoes and was now twirling barefoot in the afternoon sun.

The making-of-the-bed was to be held in her home. It was an old marriage ritual that many Portuguese had long since abandoned, especially those who lived in the larger cities. But for the women of Lomba da Maia, it was yet another opportunity to socialize and to preserve tradition, and her future mother-in-law had insisted. The house that evening had been filled with the warm smells of fresh corn-bread, and the scent of olive oil used to make sweet dough sprinkled with sugar had mixed with the warm evening air.

"But it was the smell of my mother, the way I breathed her in, that I remember the most; apricot soap with a hint of dried straw—the smell I knew I needed to carry with me to Canada."

The old sheets had been placed on Georgina's bed, and the table had been set outside for the men. Her mother moved through the house in a frenzy, sure that there was enough food, certain that the outhouse had been scrubbed and sufficiently stuffed with pine branches. She couldn't think straight, everything had to be just right. "I remember wrapping my arms around her, holding on even tighter, and breathing in deeply."

People arrived shortly thereafter. The women sat on the benches that had been brought in from the barn and placed closely against the thick earthen walls of the kitchen. For a while the men, in suits far too small for their farmers' bodies, scurried to the backyard to be with the other men, to smoke and play cards and drink.

Theresa heard a knock on the front door. She opened it and met Maria's gracious smile. It was far too large for the contempt she knew Maria felt toward this marriage.

"I saw Manuel looking over his mother's shoulder to steal a glance at me. I was carrying a tray of buttered corn-bread across the hall. It's funny the things you remember. I looked over and quickened my pace. I kissed that woman's sagging cheeks, but all the while I looked into my Manuel's round face and large blue eyes. I'll never forget how he smiled at me."

Antonio looked across the square to see where his sister had run off to. She sat on her father's lap, swung her pink feet as she tried to play his hand of cards. He resisted at first, then gave in as he always did, blew his cigarette smoke from the side of his mouth and looked over at his wife and son.

"What did he say, Georgina?" Carmen was eager to get the romantic epic back on track.

"His mother looked at Manuel sternly. It was enough to get him to fidget nervously with his tie and then head straight for the back door to meet with the other men. He tripped when he looked back at me." Georgina smiled at the recollection of her small victory.

All night, Georgina had tried to approach her future mother-in-law, but every time she got near, Grandmother Maria would turn and begin a conversation with someone beside her. They had shared a few forced smiles. But, Georgina was certain that soon the awkwardness and the contempt would have to give way to something more familial, whatever that was. "'Time has a way of doing that,' my mother used to say." Georgina shook her head, still caught in disbelief.

Grandmother Maria had entered the kitchen and sat in the corner on a low wooden stool. She pretended to read her Bible; she couldn't read and everyone knew this, but she was far too pious for anything to be said. The other women busied themselves with needlepoint or crochet. Some knitted while others enjoyed the unfolding drama.

She laid her Bible down on her lap.

"'Two weeks ago your daughter was alone, with nothing, and now . . . well, tomorrow she'll marry my son, who I already lost once. Soon, our two families will be forever bound.'" Theresa's metal crochet needles clicked faster, and stumbled as she picked up her pace.

"And then my mother stopped," Georgina said. "'*We*,' and she stressed the word while looking sideways at my future mother-in-law, 'are very happy with this blessed union.'

"'I don't know,' my mother-in-law added. 'My husband used to say that men are all barnacles. A barnacle starts out life swimming freely in the ocean. But, when it matures, it must settle down and choose a home. My dear husband used to say that it chooses to live with other barnacles of the same kind so that they can mate. He first chose Silvia . . . and then, well—' Maria stopped.

"My mother rose from her bench. Her shoulders rolled back as if ready to spring.

"'You're trying my patience, Maria.' But I moved to block my mother's step. The anger had given her the strength to push against me and move toward my mother-in-law. I pleaded with her not to ruin my night. 'I'm wasting my time with you, Maria. You have come into my home and insulted my family. For that you will pay dearly. Mark my words. You hold on to that Bible, now try to hold on to some self-respect. We have a ceremony to perform so that my daughter can marry, marry your son, and move *far away* to her new life.'

"My mother moved out of the kitchen, her long silver braid sweeping like a pendulum across her back, and slammed her bedroom door. The stress she placed on those two words, *far away*, had its desired effect. My mother-in-law's eyes turned cold. But then her frown became a smug smile."

It was the custom that each woman proceed alone to the bedroom, where she would leave a small token between the sheets, or tucked under the fitted one. There was no formal order, but it had long been understood that the young women would first bring sweet and hopeful offerings; the older women then brought symbolic gifts, usually bitter, with little or no fondness for the innocence of what was once promised them. The list of possible offerings was long; sugar sprinkled over the sheets symbolized a life of sweetness, eggs nestled under the pillows blessed the bride's fertility. Some of the scorned women brought roses: the petals reminded the bride of passion and the thorns of the pain and suffering love would inevitably bring. Each woman went in alone with her offering for the young couple.

After their offerings were placed on the bed, the younger women returned to the hot kitchen, whispered and laughed. The older women were far more reserved as their offerings and duties were performed.

The evening had been soured by what Maria had said. The women felt it in the air. It wasn't until midnight, when a few of the red-faced men came dancing into the kitchen, propping each other up, trying desperately not to topple onto the kitchen table, that the mood changed into what it was meant to be. Carmen remembered the older women halfheartedly trying to shoo the men away. Some women grabbed tea towels or the corners of their shawls to taunt them like bullfighters or flick them across their jowls or near their groins. Manuel came next, dragged on his back across the kitchen floor. Aunt Louisa recalled how Manuel's head would fall hard on the ground, but his smile was never erased. They dragged him into the bedroom and strained for the strength to swing him on top of the right side of the bed, the man's side. There wasn't even the slightest protest. Manuel had raised his head slightly from the floor and smiled dumbly. "Where's my wife-to-be?" Georgina found herself stifling her warm laughter. Some of the younger women, including Aunt Louisa and Carmen, gently led her to her side of the bed. Everyone had already crammed into the small hot room. The men finally found enough momentum to rock and swing Manuel into the air before flinging him onto the bed. At the same time, the young women pushed Georgina and she too fell backward, smiling, onto her side of the bed.

"The look on your face, Georgina," Carmen said. "The instant your body sunk into the mattress, your face twisted in pain and horror."

"It all seemed to happen so fast." Georgina's mouth trembled.

"What happened, *Mãe*? Who hurt you?" Antonio caressed her soft cheek.

"Shhhh, no one." She pressed his head close to her, kept her hand over Antonio's ear and began to rock gently.

"I remember Manuel smiling at me, ready to kiss me. But every slight move cut and tore at my back and legs. That feeling has never left me—the more I turned, the more I tried to contort my body and get up, the deeper I felt the fine pricking of my skin."

Her mother, Theresa, was the only one who recognized that something was not right. She dragged her daughter off the mattress. Georgina flopped to the floor on her knees and dropped her face into the expectant lap of her mother, who wrapped her arms around Georgina's back and muffled her sobs with her chest.

The bloody streaks that stained the sheets and blotted Georgina's new dress had silenced the room.

In horror, Manuel clumsily tore at the shredded sheets that covered the mattress. It was littered with what looked like smashed shells, glistening green shards of glass, and barnacles. Grandmother Theresa stroked her daughter's hair as her eyes searched for and landed on Grandmother Maria, who met her challenge for an instant and then sheepishly turned away. Without looking at anyone else in the room, Theresa rocked Georgina and moaned. "Get out!" she repeated. "Get out! Get out!"

After the bewildered throng spilled onto the dirt road and into their houses, Theresa spent the whole night tending to Georgina.

"She washed my back as I stood in a metal basin. She cut into her aloe plant and gently rubbed the juice on my broken skin, all the while blowing her cool breath. She hummed the same song she hummed when she used to bathe us as children, let me see, it was an old fado . . ." Here, Georgina tried to catch the first few notes of the song. Her voice cracked as she bent over and rubbed the back of her legs, where varicose veins were beginning to bud. "My mother patted dry the backs of my legs and my heels. And then she lightly wrapped my body in moistened cheesecloth, shrouded me."

The women all remained silent. Antonio did not want to move but a fly had alighted on his brow and he moved his hand slowly to brush it away and slid down his mother's legs.

"There were no words. I sobbed, still shocked at the horrible turn in the evening, as my mother dragged the damp cloth along my torn body. It's the song I can't seem to hold on to, the one my mother hummed as she took care of me by the flickering candle."

Antonio had lined up all his marbles in the grooves between the cobbled stones when Terezinha skipped up to him in her bare feet and nudged his legs. There was a choral sound of clicking glass as the marbles spilled across the square. Terezinha squatted in front of Antonio and helped him gather them. She brought Thumbelina out from under the bench, picked up a pebble and dropped it into one of her doll's legs. There was a rattling sound against the doll's hard plastic.

"We'll fill her up with rocks and then we'll bury her in the ground." Terezinha smiled at her idea. Antonio found a pebble under his shoe, reached over and dropped it into her doll.

"Make holes in her hands," Antonio suggested.

Terezinha looked pleased and began to gnaw away at her doll's fingers, tore at the loose plastic before spitting it out. "Now we can fill up her arms too." They began searching for pebbles. Antonio made sure he didn't venture too far from his mother; he didn't want to miss a word.

Aunt Louisa continued with Georgina's story, picking up seamlessly from where her sister had left off.

"The next morning, we all awoke before the cock's crow. There was such uncertainty about the day. My mother and I were both afraid to enter her room. I had tried earlier and the door had been locked. I remember my mother saying, 'She'll be fine. We always end up fine,' and as if on cue, Georgina opened her door and stepped into the kitchen with her wedding dress half on, the bodice flapped in front of her like a bib.

"Georgina reached into the flared sleeves of her dress, turned her back to us and said, '*Mãe*, help me pull up the dress.' Her back was covered . . . we looked down and saw that some of the blood from the backs of her legs had already been blotted by her white nylons.

"'Oh, *filha*, this can wait. Things have changed and you . . . ' my mother cried.

"'Nothing has changed.' Georgina turned her face toward us and smiled. I'll never forget it."

Carmen looked at Georgina and made the sign of the cross. The bells of the church began to ring. Antonio looked at his mother just as she remembered the first few bars of the fado and began to sing.

> Don't cry my little one,
> your pretty friends of glass and clay
> sit on your windowsill at night,
> playful in the day.

The other women now recognized the lullaby. They smiled and joined in the singing.

> The winds may blow,
> sending them tumbling down,
> but the love I have,
> the love you need from me,
> will always be there.

Even Terezinha dropped her doll. It was as if the whole square had stopped, frozen in space and time. Antonio shaded his eyes from the brilliant sky and saw his father shift awkwardly and move in their direction. Antonio tugged at his mother's dress, tried to warn her of his father's advance. She knew. She saw.

"'There's nothing for you here!' my mother said. It was with those words that I took my first step into the church and then the next step. I saw the woman who was to be my mother-in-law at the end of the aisle and I fought my pain. I held on to my mother's hand and we walked toward the altar together, toward Manuel."

Carmen now reflected on what she had seen. "We were all so quiet, the church was so silent. Frankly, we couldn't believe what we were seeing. You were smiling and you walked so gracefully, as if hovering across that aisle toward Manuel. I think we felt shame for what had happened. You passed with your proud mother, Louisa here was crying as she held your long beautiful train. And then we were silenced. It was only when you passed that we could see the traces of blood through the fabric of your dress; red blotches covered your back and legs, seeped through the satin and lace."

Carmen looked down at Terezinha, who sat beside her now, and whispered, "Your mother was a vision—so beautiful."

Terezinha nuzzled her cheek against Georgina's arm. Antonio stood in front of his mother and faced his father's shadow as it blocked the sun.

"Georgina, what is all this prattling so soon after my mother's death. Laughing and singing, have you no respect?"

Antonio noticed how his father's buttoned white collar stood in sharp contrast to his red neck and face.

Georgina raised her arms slightly before anyone could protest.

"I remember looking to my side, seeing that woman, Maria Theresa da Conceição Rebelo. Padre Jose opened with an invitation for the family blessing. Manuel kissed my mother and asked for her blessing. My mother later said she had seen into his eyes saw how genuinely sorry he was and whispered, 'Never come back. Take my *filha,* but never come back.' Remember, Manuel?" she asked.

Manuel stood defeated.

"Manuel looked at me then and I smiled at him. Without hesitation, I turned toward his mother, who refused to rise from her pew. The congregation held its breath. I bent down low to meet my new mother-in-law and her smell of mothballs. I held my breath and kissed her on both stone cheeks, then held her tight in an embrace."

Georgina raised her face to meet her husband's. He bowed his head.

"'He's dead to you.' I whispered it so only she could hear. 'As God is my witness, you will never see your son again. He's dead to you.' And I smiled. I remember hearing the roar and the applause that filled the church. I straightened, my stiff dress shifted across my cuts, pulled at my searing wounds. I held on to Manuel's hand. I turned my crimson back to the crowd, to this backward little village of Lomba da Maia, and I solemnized my vows."

~ II ~

CAGED BIRDS SING

But a bird that stalks down his narrow cage
can seldom see through his bars of rage
his wings are clipped and his feet are tied
so he opens his throat to sing . . .

The caged bird sings with fearful trill
of the things unknown but longed for still
and his tune is heard on the distant hill
for the caged bird sings of freedom

Maya Angelou

~ *URBAN ANGEL* ~

MY FATHER DEMANDED WE all speak English. "We is in Canada now. We speak Canadian in this beautiful country with many beautiful things," he'd say. He was so certain of his chosen land that I couldn't help but love him. I just wished he would use a word other than *beautiful,* which he pronounced *bootiful.* He had been promising to take the family on a cross-country train ride for as long as I could remember—to see the country as he had. He was proud of his early days working on the railway, walking the lines like the Johnny Cash song he couldn't stop humming. My father never stopped talking about lakes and rivers with long Indian names. My mother tried unsuccessfully to pronounce some of the places—Chilliwack, Coquitlam, Saskatchewan—all in the hopes of pleasing my father.

The nuns who ran St. Michael's Hospital and who first hired my father told my mother how impressed they had been with his valiant attempts at English and his determined work ethic, not to mention his blue eyes and long lashes. "Too gorgeous," they would say to her, "to be placed in the head of a man." The nuns chose to hire him without any experience. Under Sister Ophelia's tutelage, my father mopped, scrubbed, and disinfected for only a short while before he was proclaimed supervisor of the hospital's housekeeping department. It was a meteoric rise, or so my mother would proudly say. He had an office. It was located in the basement.

"Remember, I is a supervisor," he'd announce, puffed chest and all. It was made clear to us that if ever asked we were never to reveal what exactly he was a supervisor of. It was a family secret, just like all the employee evaluations he could never fill out for himself. Misplaced glasses or a terrible headache would always lead him in our direction. My sister would roll her eyes as she typed up the forms. My father pretended not to notice. My mother would take us aside and again remind us, "What happens in this house, stays in this house."

I was struggling with her shaky rule about keeping things within the confines of our home when I caught my Aunt Louisa smuggling piecework—stacks of pockets to be sewn on the backs of jeans—upstairs, into my mother's workroom. My mother shushed me. "I'm helping your *tia*," she said. "We need the extra bit of money." I proudly skipped downstairs and whispered what my mother was doing into my father's ear. His feet hammered up the stairs. He reappeared at the top of the stairwell trailed by my mother, who tugged at his shirt with one hand and

with the other hand tried to grab the jumble of jeans he
carried in his arms. My mother flung the jeans she had
managed to tear from his grasp over her shoulder and
bent to pick up the pants that had fallen.

He went outside, red-faced and barefoot in the
snow, and threw the jeans into a heap, kicked at them to
pile them higher. He disappeared into the garage and,
when he returned, squirted barbecue starter fluid all
over the mound. My mother tried to drag what she could
away before he lit a match and flicked it on the pile. She
shielded her face from the ball of instant blue then
orange flame. In front of the blazing pyre she stood,
panting with strands of hair lodged in the corners of her
mouth. My father stood behind the flames, his torso and
face awash with a warm glow. My mother turned. She
zipped her housecoat up and down so fast her fist
blurred. She stopped, caught me looking through the
screen door. She allowed her eyelids to shut, then tilted
her chin to the sky.

My mother and what seemed like most of my family
worked at St. Michael's Hospital, amid the glass buildings in the center of the city. Every time I entered the
building I would go directly to the statue of Michael the
Archangel and sit under his large stone wings. The nuns
who ran the hospital had told my father they had purchased the marble statue for forty-eight dollars and that
it was carved out of the same marble as the *Pietà*. "That
statue is in the Vatican," my father would say. The statue
of Michael stood in the hospital's Bond Street entrance—

"the urban angel," that's what they called the hospital. I
liked to think people called it that because of the statue
that looked down on everyone who was rushed through
the corridors strapped to their blood-soaked gurneys.
Almost every drug overdose, stabbing, shooting, or
attempted suicide was brought there first. I liked to think
it was Michael that decided who was worthy of getting
fixed—who deserved a second chance.

I was almost ten when I first spoke to the archangel.
With hands pressed together, palm to palm, I began with
three Our Fathers and five Hail Marys.

"Angel Michael, can you hear me?" I asked with my
lips slightly parted, just like a ventriloquist. There were
people walking through the halls and I didn't want anyone to hear. "Can you just pretend I'm on my knees? I
know that I'm not always the best kid, the best son, but
I want to be good." I looked over my shoulder. "This
summer I'm going to stop stealing: chocolate bars and
gum from Senhora Rosa's variety store, and bikes; I'll tell
Manny I don't want to help him steal bikes anymore. It's
not worth the five bucks Senhor Alfredo's son gives us. I
promise to keep secrets—those that can hurt people, at
least. I've been trying really hard because my mother says
that's the only way I can be an angel of God—like you.
Oh! And the wings"—I had almost forgotten—"for the
festa; I've been praying for so long now, please, please,
help me get chosen. I promise to be good . . . as good as I
can be. In the name of the Father and . . ."

I got off the elevator and turned the corner before
opening my father's door. There was a small waiting
room and I sat in one of the mismatched chairs. I could

hear noises coming from inside his office. I tried to push open the door, even kicked it once.

"*Pai,* it's me. Are you in there?"

I was leaning against the door when it sprang open. I fell in. Sister Ophelia, who had given my father the job at the hospital, looked at me with squinted eyes that narrowed her nose like a pencil. I had always liked Sister Ophelia. Every Christmas my father would bring home a picture of him and the nuns gathered around the hospital's fake Christmas tree. While all the other nuns looked stiff in their pressed cotton shirts, their long skirts and rubber-soled shoes, Sister Ophelia looked fresh, as if she had run across a field of wildflowers in slow motion like in that commercial for some kind of feminine product my sister could never really explain to me. Sister Ophelia wore pumps, and the hem of her skirt sat just above her knees. But most scandalous of all was the faint outline of a bra you could clearly see beneath her creamy chiffon blouse. She always stood next to my father in these pictures, and I couldn't help but notice she was taller than him.

My father's face was flushed as Sister Ophelia searched for her glasses on his desk. The white buttons on her blouse didn't match up and the gaping pucker went unnoticed by her. She placed the glasses on the sharp ridge of her nose and moved toward me with a firm step. Her heels clickety-clacked on the linoleum. I was about to say hello but stopped when she looked down at me with her laser eyes. I curled into a ball as she stepped over me. She twisted her hair into a bun before making a sharp turn at the door.

My father sat under a large photograph of a swooshing train that blurred into the distance: CANADIAN PACIFIC.

"Never! Never come and disturb my work."

"But *Pai*, I was . . ."

My father raised his hand. "Where did I tell you to meet? Huh, where?"

The top of his bald head shone like a mirror; I could see the reflection of the fluorescent bulbs that hung in his office, two neat rows.

"Get out! Get out of here! Leave! Go see you . . . mother."

I ran out of his office and up the stairs. I ran down the corridor, funneled through the sickening dark halls and past the statue before punching my way through the doors and jumping six stairs to the sidewalk on Bond Street. I sucked in the cold air and breathed in my secret. I didn't take the streetcar home, just ran across Queen Street, past the neon lights of Yonge Street, University Avenue and the fountains, Spadina and all the boarded-up storefronts, then Bathurst and turned up Palmerston Avenue. I made it all the way home without stepping on any cracks.

The winter was slipping away and the yellow grass was beginning to show blotches of green. My father was in a terrible mood. He was home most days but he hardly spoke to anyone and looked away when I came into the room. He avoided the front door, chose to enter through the garage and then down into the house through the basement. I could see that it concerned my

mother. He had stopped going to work and people were
asking questions. Every time she tried to talk to him
about it, he would mumble something then leave to tend
to his pigeons or piddle around with his gardening hoe
in the still-frozen soil. My sister would look to my
mother for an answer. "Leave your father alone for a
while." I said nothing, betrayed no one.

At the end of March, my father came home with a
terrific grin on his face. He rounded us all up and
directed us to the front stoop. My mother was thrilled to
see this change in him. We shuffled excitedly down the
hallway as if it were a game. My father bolted ahead of us
as we came out and leaned his back against the shiny red
cab of a huge dump truck parked in front of our home.
He had his arms crossed, a chamois that knotted like a
pretzel in front of his chest peeking through. He smiled
as he moved away from the door and with the side of his
open hand sawed back and forth under large gold letters
set in an arch: MANUEL AND SONS HAULAGE CO. Our
phone number was printed underneath.

"What did you do, Manuel?"

My father looked up and down the street before kicking a tire hard.

My mother asked in a whisper, "How much did
this cost?"

He spun around. "It's always about the money. If
you're going to make it in this country you don't ask
how much things cost." He spiked the chamois onto the
sidewalk.

My mother looked up and down the street, scouring
for neighbors.

"Did my cousin ask how much things cost when his bakery business took off?"

This was going to be my father's next attempt at "making it," a dump truck operation. Before that there had been the goat cheese business he had bought into with his cousin, until they couldn't get a goat's milk supplier and he was forced to bail out of the venture. He tried to make pigeon breeding a career but didn't understand it was a hobby based on bartering and trading—not on making money. He sold sets of non-stick pots and pans door to door, then vacuum cleaners, until he settled on sheet sets and sateen bedspreads sold from his car. His latest venture had ended last week. He'd had a home cleaning business on the side—local banks at night, which evolved into cleaning homes in Rosedale and Forest Hill. That was going well until the police came to our house during March break looking for certain detergents and cleaning items that had been clearly stamped ST. MICHAEL'S HOSPITAL. I was the only one at home with my father when they searched the basement and the trunk of his car and confiscated everything. I never said anything to anyone.

"Manuel, you left your job last week. You won't talk to me and I don't have the answers. Everyone at work has been asking where you are and now . . . Sister Ophelia says you were . . . let go. Why, Manuel? Answer me, what happened at work?" Her lips fluttered as if little sparrows were flying out of her mouth. I looked over. My sister didn't seem to react.

"You hold me back!" He pointed his finger at my mother but looked straight at me. A string of spit clung to his chin. "It's because of you that I've gone nowhere!"

My sister put her arm around my mother's waist as her limp figure slipped back into the house. My father's arm, the same one that shook as he pointed at her, dropped and slapped his side.

I stood alone on the veranda.

"*Filho,* climb in." These were the first words he had spoken to me in over a week. "I did this for us, *filho.* For you."

I turned and went inside the house.

I hated Saturday mornings, especially when the weather was beginning to get so nice. While other kids played on the street or in the laneways shared by Palmerston Avenue and Markham Street, I had to put on my dress clothes, a large felt cross pinned to my chest. My mother had signed me up for catechism that spring. She thought I'd stay out of trouble, away from my hoodlum friends—and who knew, maybe I'd even learn the Beatitudes.

"You look nice—a proper Soldier of God." My mother smiled.

My father sat at the kitchen table, cracking walnuts between his fingers, two at a time.

"Manuel, look at your son. Isn't he handsome?" My mother said. The words they shared had been few since my father bought the truck and lost his job at the hospital. My mother had attempted to smooth things over, punctuating the days with inoffensive comments or supportive observations. My father still couldn't look at me for very long.

"He's a good boy. He doesn't need to look like the

navio that Columbus sailed, with that cross pinned to his chest."

"Manuel, don't . . ."

"Don't you . . ." He slammed his fist hard. The walnuts rolled, then tumbled onto the kitchen floor. Their bumpy shells sounded like rattlesnakes as they spread across the linoleum. He regained his composure, quietly got up and walked to the back door. He turned to my mother. She didn't look up at him, just bent down and gathered the walnuts into her apron. I got on my knees and helped.

"I don't want my children kissing the Pope's ass!" Then, after a slight pause, he continued. "He's Canadian. Leave Portuguese things back home for the old to die with." The room was quiet. "I don't want him bowing at the dirty feet of a priest."

My father had always resented the priests at our parish—all priests, in fact—and for the most part stayed away from Sunday mass. My mother never seemed to mind; he had his reasons, as far as she was concerned, and she used the peaceful hour at mass every week to collect her thoughts.

I ran all the way, slipping every so often in my new shoes, until I found myself on the front steps of St. Mary's Church, Portugal Square.

I entered into the darkness of the church. It always smelled like Lemon Pledge. I tried to pat down my cowlick with the holy water before pushing open the heavy green doors. I always liked the hollow sound my

shoes made walking up the aisle, the way every step or
lowering of the kneeler reverberated throughout the old
church. Heads turned as I walked up the aisle toward
Sister Pedrosa, who met me with her almond eyes and
flaring nostrils. We used to aim peashooters at her nose.
Mulched pieces of paper towel were chewed then molded
into tiny pellets before our tongues stuffed them wet and
hard into straws. A quick burst of air sent the projectile
close to, if not up, the cavernous walls of Sister's nose as
she stood in front of the altar. Manny actually hit it once,
just as the sister tilted her head back in praise of God.
Tears welled in her eyes before she ran out of the church.
I think people felt bad. I didn't care.

"Antonio." Her upper and lower jaws moved in
opposite directions as if she was chewing something.
"Why are you late?"

"I had diarrhea, Sister. So when I went to the bathroom . . ." I pulled at the back of my pants for added
effect.

Her hand came up, stopped me. Some girls began to
laugh.

"Sorry, Sister, I didn't know *diarrhea* was a bad word."

"Just sit!"

Everyone noticed my victory smirk as I sidestepped
along the pew toward Ricky and sat down. I flicked his
shoulder; he turned and smiled without really looking at
me. Things had been like this between us now for a
while. A couple of weeks back, as my boots splashed in
the puddles that dotted our laneway, I came across Ricky,
who crouched near the heating vents at the rear of
Senhor Jerome's Pool Hall.

"Hey, Ricky! What's up?" I had shouted.

He had fumbled a bit, reluctantly turned to face me. Steam shot from his nose and mouth. He staggered in the mist then took off, just clear took off around the corner and out onto Markham Street.

I was about to follow but a scratching sound, like dog nails on concrete, made me turn toward the fence. I saw nothing but a hole the size of a pickle jar lid cut into the fence that I knew shaded the outdoor patio where the men drank and played cards. I saw a flash of blue paper being dropped, an eyeball darting from side to side. I moved closer, squatted to pick up the five-dollar bill folded lengthwise in a V. Then a penis poked its way through the hole—its purple head bobbed on a shaft held by nicotine-stained fingers. I scrambled to my feet and ran, all the way down the lane and into my garage. I closed my eyes to collect my thoughts. I could hear my heart pounding.

Ricky hadn't been at school for a while; he was often absent. But a week later he came over to speak to me.

"Sorry I ran from you last week," he said.

"Did I scare you?"

"Nah, it's just . . . well, I was . . . what did you want anyways?"

"Nothing. I tried to follow you but you were too fast for me." I smiled. I liked the feeling of hoarding secrets.

Ricky ran his fingers through his curly hair; half moons of dirt lay under his fingernails. Manny had told me Ricky's dad was out of work. I never believed it; Ricky's pockets always seemed too full. Five-dollar bills, all rolled or crumpled into tight balls, would spill out of his pocket whenever he'd treat us all to Surprise Bags, Black Cat gum, or Lola's. We weren't allowed to hang around at his house. "My father works at night and he gets terrible migraines. I'm not allowed to have friends over." Ricky intrigued me; it was as if he lived alone without anyone to care for him. But he seemed happy.

"As I was saying, children, the *Festa do Senhor Santo Cristo* is almost here, the most important feast of the year. I've made my decisions. After I call out your names please make sure that you pick up your costumes from the rectory before going home today." We all wanted to be the Angel Michael in the procession. We all wanted those massive wings. The wired halo, sparkling with crystals that jiggled in the sunlight, was a small price to pay for the sword the Angel brandished. This was to be my year. I had prayed to the Angel Michael for months. I had kept my secrets and prayed for my father, and for Ricky too. Angel Michael had heard me, he had seen the change and I was sure to be rewarded.

"Ahem." Sister cleared her throat to announce this was it. "This year, Angel Michael will be played by . . ."—she scanned the room for teasing effect and her eyes landed on me—"Ricardo Mendonca." Sister Pedrosa looked pleased with herself. In the midst of all the congratulatory noise and my stunned silence, I managed to wriggle my hand out from my lint-filled pocket. I patted Ricky on his shoulder. He seemed shocked by the decision. A crowd huddled around him but I managed to loosen myself from the knot—to move away from everyone's praise, Sister Pedrosa's smugness and evil nostrils. I made my way to the large wooden doors. The faint wisps of incense seared the back of my throat. I sat outside on the church's stone steps and sucked in a blast of cool spring air.

I walked home with my paltry wings fit only for a worthless, nameless angel, feathers flattened and worn. I had turned back a couple of times and caught a glimpse of Ricky. The fluffy white feathers of his wings flittered with the slightest breeze, and the sword tucked in his belt flashed in the sunlight. I tried to walk faster. The thought of trailing behind Ricky under the shade of his wings for the entire parade made me crazy. Sister Pedrosa had made a mistake. She didn't know what kind of boy Ricky really was.

Ricky walked quickly behind me up Tecumseth Street, past the incredible smell of bread in the oven drifting over from Future Bakery. I stopped at the Queen Street crosswalk then hurried to the north side, Palmerston Avenue. I knew Ricky was running to catch up to me; I could hear him calling my name, to stop. I pictured him holding his big beautiful wings and quickened my pace.

"Listen, Antonio, it's not my fault that . . ." He moved in front of me and tried to catch his breath.

"Those should be mine!" I blurted.

"Who says?"

"Angel Michael told me so." I tried to catch the words but they rolled off my tongue.

His eyes widened. "What are you talking about?"

I tried to pass him but he held on to my arm.

"*Who* told you?" Ricky asked. His cheeks began to tremble with laughter. "You're nuts."

"You want to talk about nuts! They serve nuts at the pool hall, don't they, Ricky? . . . You want to talk about that?" Spit sprayed from my mouth. I had said too much.

Ricky dropped his magnificent wings and lunged at me. There was part of me that wished he had ripped his sword from its sheath and waved it over his head. But his attack was halfhearted. He drove his head into my chest, as if he had already lost. My fingers rolled and tangled in his hair. It was all I could grab hold of as a short gust caught my wings. I looked over my shoulder, reluctant to give up the hold I had on him. He snorted against my chest, his face wet. My wings skittered and flapped onto Queen Street, and finally came to rest on the streetcar tracks. I watched as the red blur of the streetcar cut over them.

I saw a different kind of horror in Ricky's eyes. I let go, scraped him off me like a clinging scab, and dodged the traffic to get my wings. I gathered the dissected pieces of wire, torn cardboard, and bald patches where feathers once had been and lifted them over my head. Cars stopped and honked. Some man craned his neck out a window. "Get off the road!" I turned and flipped him the bird.

I dragged my mangled wings to the sidewalk. Ricky knelt on the sidewalk and looked at me with his snotty face. "Now look what you've done!" I said. He sat back on his heels, then moved his dirty hands and fingernails to his face.

When my mother returned from trying to explain the unfortunate accident with the wings to Sister Pedrosa, she was angry. She said nothing until after dinner once my sister and I had gone to bed. I sat at the top of the stairs and looked between the spindles at my mother slowly clearing the table in a cloud of smoke. My father leaned against the counter with a cigarette and took long casual drags.

"Then she said . . ."—my mother looked into the air as if she were trying to catch a bug—"a boy like that needs to understand respect. Can you believe it? Then she tells me we owe the church twenty-four dollars. I mean, where does she get the nerve."

"Judgment and money. One they give; the other they steal." My father said these words without any energy. He didn't care.

My mother stopped scrubbing a pot. She wiped her hands along her rooster-trimmed apron, palms first, then the backs of her hands across her thighs. She spun around to face my father. I clenched my teeth and closed my eyes in prayer—*Please don't start. Let it go, Mãe.* I heard the back door slam and when I opened my eyes my mother stood under the kitchen light, alone.

I ran to my room and looked out my window, which had a clear view of the backyard. My father flicked the light switch and walked into the aviary he had built to house his prized white fancy pigeons. I knelt by my bed and whispered, "Angel Michael . . . I just wanted some wings. It was all I wanted for keeping the secrets. I'll be good, I promise. Amen."

That night my sleep was pierced by violent squawks and sudden outbursts of frantic and rhythmic cooing. The next morning, I awoke to the reek of burning hair.

My mother stood bent over the stove, singeing the feathered stubble from the pimply gray flesh over the blue flame. A heap of pigeons lay on the kitchen table. I thought of raccoons. My father had caught one trying to get into the aviary last week. He had drowned it in the laundry tubs in the basement; I had watched the trapped animal poke its human-like hands through the cage and desperately ram its snout through one of the holes.

"*Mãe*, where's Dad?" I asked.

My mother turned to me with her dark, tired eyes, gave me a half-smile but didn't answer. She just kept rolling the small birds—two fingers pinching their beaks, her other fingers holding their feet—over the gas flame. She stopped every so often and rubbed her forehead with a scrunched shoulder, absorbed in her work.

Three weeks later and it was the *festa* weekend. I wanted to stay in bed all day. I came downstairs to raid the refrigerator and then barricade myself in my room.

That's when I saw them.

You couldn't miss them. Massive wings. They sat in their new back harness, tall and graceful in the center of the kitchen table. Their tips almost touched the ceiling. I circled the table a few times, daring to brush my fingertips lightly across their softness. I knew at once they were there for me. I dropped hard to my knees, looked up at my glowing new wings.

"Hail Mary, full of Grace, The Lord is with Thee . . ."

I heard the front door open and quickly stood up. I knew that my father had driven my mother to morning mass. My mother came in and paused for a moment. She gently shut the door then looked at me. Her eyes then scanned the wings. She pulled off her white gloves, exposing their gray, stained insides.

"Where's *Pai?*"

"Putting the car in the garage." She considered their magnificence, held her fingers to her lips in awe.

There was joy beaming from her tired body. She removed her sweater, turned to get the multicolored housecoat she had bought at Kensington Market, zipped it up, blew her nose, and stuffed the front pockets with Kleenex.

"Your clothes are ready. They're in your closet. Go wash up. We don't want to be late for the procession."

I turned to go upstairs as my mother circled the kitchen table, moving closer to study the wings. She held a fist to her mouth. I took two steps then stopped to look at my glorious wings again.

Ricky's going to be pissed.

My father had covered the wings with a few garbage bags so that he could deliver them safely to the church. He had put them in the back of his truck and gently tied them down with string. My mother and I sat silently in the cab as he drove toward church.

We were to get ready in the basement of the church hall. The only reason my father was there was because he wanted to carry the wings himself, afraid they would break or get damaged. Otherwise, he would have been home, covering the tomato seedlings with glass jars and digging up the fig tree that he buried every year in the dark earth, making it stand again for another year of growth. Sister Pedrosa saw us and approached like a snorting bull as she clapped her hands together to shoo us like field hens.

"What is going on here?"

"Are we late, Sister?" my mother began. "I'm so sorry that . . ."

My father carefully lifted the dark green bags from my wings. I heard the rush of gasps turn into a collective hush. I reached up high, smiled and touched their arching tips.

"*Não!* He can't wear those in the *procissão!* They're too large and Ricardo has been chosen. Ricardo is Archangel Michael and those wings are too large. I'm sorry if this has caused any embarrassment but—" She turned to walk away, shaking her hands in the air as if wiping them clean.

"He will wear them!" my father shouted.

My mother looked at him, pressed her hand against his chest. It gave him strength, a clear and passionate voice.

"He will be an angel in this parade and no one will stop him."

My mother looked down at me, smiled and brushed the hair away from my eyes. Sister Pedrosa stopped in her tracks for only a moment. She then continued her march toward the rectory, certain to find a sympathetic audience there.

I could see Ricky standing on a chair alone. Sister Pedrosa had been hemming his long white robe. He stepped down and walked with his head low across the creaky floor. The sounds had slowly come alive again.

He stopped in front of me. He smiled, raised the halo off his head, and moved to place it on mine.

"No, Ricky—you're Michael," I said.

Ricky helped with the straps as my father struggled to adjust the wings on my back.

The moment we moved outside and onto Adelaide Street, my eyes adjusted to the sun's glare and my body teetered with the weight on my back. I paced in front of the women who walked barefoot, some on their knees for the whole two-kilometer stretch, fulfilling their vows, their *promessas*—promises. They would begin to drop back and reach the church at night, but their pain would have left them a long time before, I thought. Or was the pain with them, a reminder of why they came, the sacrifice they made in order to get something in return? Behind me was the figure of *Senhor Santo Cristo dos Milagres,* his legs crossed on a cloud of plastic flowers. He seemed so small, covered in his bejeweled red velvet cloak. The large crown of thorns pierced his temples and the trickles of blood fringed his forehead and ran along his cheeks and down his tensed neck. The people who decorated him every year, adorned him with ribbons of gold and buckets of plastic flowers, made him look larger than he really was. As the statue passed, the thousands that lined Adelaide and Richmond streets genuflected and made signs of the cross in a wave. Children were nudged, pinched, or slapped into doing the same.

I had to keep in step, although it became increasingly difficult with the wind that hit me when I turned west onto Richmond Street. But I kept going, shuffling along the street strewn with real petals and dyed sawdust, looking at the colorful hooked carpets or bedspreads that hung from windows or wrought-iron railings. Bands played and we stepped in unison with the rhythm.

Some feathers fell to the ground. With every labored step more feathers would drop from my wings. Ricky looked back a few times and smiled. The last time he didn't look at me, but at the tips of my wings. He seemed concerned. I looked over my shoulder and saw a freshly exposed area. I could make out a trace of CCM in red on the wooden frame that held my wings towering over my head.

In my mind I saw my mother's gray eyes, my father's chafed fingers, the pile of dead pigeons, the hockey sticks that were meant to hold our tomatoes that summer.

Every time a gust of wind caught my wings, challenging my balance, I thought of what it all meant and with a firm resolve straightened myself, shifted and adjusted the weight on my sore shoulders, over my weakening knees, until we made it to the church steps.

God listens to your prayers if your knees hurt a little.

I turned proudly to face the crowd. As I scanned the throng from the top of the church steps, I caught my mother's wave. She raised her hand, placed it on her head, and shifted her black lace veil over her face. I saw my father making his way through the crowd, away from the church steps. He was the only one wearing a hat. I knew he wouldn't stay for the mass. When he broke into open space, he turned to face me. I puffed air into my chest, threw my tired shoulders back, held the wings strong and straight. He began to walk up Bathurst Street with his straw hat, a feather tucked into its ribboned trim.

"Ricky! Let's go." I grabbed Ricky's hand and we wove our way down the steps and through the humming crowd, pushed sideways with our shoulders. Ricky raised his plastic sword and cut his way through. The crowd smiled at what they thought was a carefully choreographed liturgical dance. My magnificent wings only widened the path until we came to a clearing on Bathurst, past the orange barricades. We caught up to my father, who had parked the truck in front of Corrado's barbershop. His knee was raised, about to climb into the cab of his new truck.

"Can we ride in the back, *Pai*?" I asked.

He was about to say something but the words didn't come out. He simply smiled and nodded.

We climbed up to the dumper, scampered through the rocks, dirt, and brick on our way to the top of the mound. Mindful of the rusted rebar that cracked the dirty surface like urban stalagmites, we planted our feet firmly, level with the rim of the dumper. My father revved the engine, then it kicked into gear. We moved slowly up Bathurst. He pulled the chain and released the deep honk from the belly of his truck. I turned back to see Padre Nunes splash holy water across the crowd in a final blessing. I grabbed Ricky's hand and we locked our fingers together. He drew the sword from its sheath with his free hand and offered it to me. I took hold of it, stabbed the sword deep into the rubble and rested my hand on the handle to steady myself. My father turned and I could see his bobbing round face and blue eyes

through a window at the back of the cab. A breath of
wind curled around my legs, hit the underside of my
graceful wings with such force that as I looked up into
the pale sky I could feel a lightness run through my body,
feel my toes lift off the dirt, my head bobbing above
Ricky's. If only a few inches—if for only a few seconds.

~ *SHOESHINE BOY* ~

"IF YOU FEET NO SIT RIGHT on pedals, even little wrong, you can lose balance, fall and hurt youself."

With my left properly placed on the pedal, I skipped with my right foot and hopped onto the padded banana seat.

"Okay—you is okay." I could hear my father encouraging me.

I could hear his urging: "Balance! . . . Balance! No hurt youself!" His fading voice mixed with the warm wind humming in my ears.

I was six then. As I grew older I ventured farther, past Senhora Rosa's variety store where colored balls and blinking dolls wrapped in cellophane dangled from invisible strings tacked to the yellowed ceiling. Everything twisted and twirled every time I made my way into the store, pushing the large "Coke" handle and tripping the familiar chime. I pedaled to the clicking of colored straws that covered my spokes, all the way to the top of our street to the synagogue, "da church for Jewish peoples," and onto Dundas Street with the blur of the Red Rockets. That's where I stopped.

By the age of seven, Palmerston, Markham, and Euclid Avenue all bored me. Manny had coined it "Name That House!" I'd call out a number and he would tell me the color of its brick: pink, blue, or lime green. For some, we were even able to name who lived there.

"86 Euclid?" I'd shout.

"Yellow with green porch, aluminum awning, Mr. Almeida by himself, breeds canaries." A slight pause then, "Cheesy fingers—Rothmans!"

Manny was amazing. He had it right down to the brand.

When things got that predictable we moved on to new adventures, to the backs of our houses. I pedaled through the intricate labyrinth of laneways, with their crooked garage roofs, dark gurgling gutters, and tangled clotheslines. We would ride our bikes across the cracked and uneven concrete, dodging sewer grates and peeling out from gravel patches. Some nooks in the laneways had been good places to dump garbage: old shoes, a wedding dress, shopping carts, a wig, worn tires.

By age ten I knew everything about where I lived, every picket and dented door, the pitch of every mother's call when the streetlights came on and we scurried onto our verandas and then into our dimly lit homes like ants disappearing into sand holes. After a storm, I knew how the water ran from the garage spouts toward the center of our lane, how these small murky streams would meet and mix with spots of gasoline that dotted our laneway. Once together the colorful blue and violet film would swirl and gather before picking up speed and dumping itself into the storm sewer. We used to enjoy racing twigs or cigarette butts, anything that could float. We'd squat at the top of these alley creeks, name our men, and then drop them into the speeding rivulet. We'd run alongside, cheering.

I felt safe growing up. I was comforted by what I knew, what was familiar. It was only at night that the alley became sinister. I had a recurring nightmare that someone was trying to hurt me . . . *I dropped my bike and ran barefoot down my laneway. Small stones and shards of glass cut into my dirty feet. I couldn't look back at their faces. I ran, opened my hands and chopped the wind in front of me. I could hear them breathing, mocking, "You, boy, with the pretty hair. Why don't you come in, got something I'd like to share." The words swam inside my head like minnows, tickled my brain: "little boy with the pretty hair" . . .*

It took the summer that no one slept—the summer my family butchered a pig and Emanuel Jaques, the shoeshine boy, went missing—to realize the words my father had used to cushion me, *balance* and *no hurt*, and the place I knew so well could no longer protect me.

~

I would wake up in the morning to the whir of my sister's blow-dryer mixed with Streisand's "Evergreen" or the high-pitched vocals of the Bee Gees' "How Deep Is Your Love" blaring in the background. She was sixteen and in a couple of weeks I'd be twelve, and that was one year before officially becoming a teenager, something I felt I was quite qualified to be considering only a week before I had found a hair between my legs—the first.

My sister and I lived in separate worlds: she stayed on the phone for hours, watching TV and listening to CHUM, all at the same time. I chose to spend my summer outside where I could get on my bike and pedal up the street to see Manny or Dennis, to trade hockey cards, play nearest-to-the-wall or buck-buck, or hop from one garage rooftop to the next all the way up the laneway. We'd take a break outside Senhora Rosa's store and cool off with a Lola. Our bikes were our constant companions, our ticket to the world beyond our street and our neighborhood.

"Maybe that's what he was doing," Manny said.

"Who?" I asked, sucking on the now white ice of my grape Lola.

"Emanuel. He was working on Yonge Street shining shoes so that he could buy a new bike!" Manny was pleased with himself.

"What, and he never came back? No . . . I don't think so. You know they're saying he did things . . . for money. And it wasn't shining shoes."

"No," Manny said. "I don't believe what they say. I *know* he just rode away and didn't want to come back."

I wanted to believe Manny was right. Like Emanuel, all we wanted was an escape from our little Portuguese neighborhood. We wanted our mothers to buy peanut butter, Swanson TV dinners, and macaroni and cheese. We wanted our mothers to drive—to summer camp or the

Eaton Centre. We wanted our fathers to wear shirts and
ties to work. We wanted them to go to the park and play
with us, kick a soccer ball around. But there was always
work, and then the other work they went to after dinner.
If there was any time left over, it was used to fix the house
and tend the gardens. It seemed we measured everything
by time, or the lack of it. And we didn't want to inter-
pret, at the bank or when someone rang the doorbell
selling Electrolux vacuum cleaners. We were tired of
responding to the teasing of schoolmates—"No! We don't
eat fish every day!"—with clenched teeth. Some of us had
already found ways to fight what it was we were supposed
to be; my sister had gone from Terezinha to Terri, with
an *i*, and even though my name was registered at school
as Antonio, teachers always took the liberty on that first
day of calling out Tony, and I never corrected them.

For our parents, Palmerston Avenue *was* "back
home." Nothing had ever really changed. There were
always eyes behind curtained windows, like those of
Senhora Gloria, who saw and heard and thrived on all
things seen and heard. Fados sifted through screen doors,
the smell of barbecued sardines wove through the chain-
link fences, and colorful clothing and bleached towels
flapped in the warm wind until they were hard and
crunchy on the clotheslines. Our backyards were contra-
dictions, with their neat rows of beans and tomatoes and
kale propped up by a mishmash of weathered dowels, old
hockey sticks, and scraps of quarter-round. Nothing was
ever thrown out. Everything was to be used. Squirrels and
raccoons were supposedly deterred by a series of tin cans
filled with dried beans, or the rattle of nails against tin

pie plates suspended with twine. Large dill pickle jars sheltered the tender tomato plants from the unpredictable frost. My mother's old pantyhose were used to tie the long bean plants on their rapid ascent. Even the large trout or bass that our neighbor Mr. Barber kindly offered my father—my mother insisted the man he lived with who lisped and wore outrageous shirts, Mr. Wolenska, was his brother—was always received with a smile and thanks, only to be whisked to the backyard where it was buried in the garden to be used as fertilizer. My father was convinced that lake fish weren't good to eat, they didn't have the natural sea salt that kept other fish healthy and free from disease and pollutants.

It was an annual event—*a matança*—the killing. This was the kind of thing that embarrassed me; here we were in a big city with butcher shops throughout Kensington Market and yet the farmer mentality brought over from the Azores had survived.

I watched as they dragged the pig from the dumper of my father's truck and tied its hind legs with rope. The tongue lolled outside the pig's mouth, its pinkness dragging on the dirty floor. Its snout was brown with gravel and sand. My Uncle David's garage door was up so all our neighbors could see. He lived only three houses down from us on Palmerston Avenue, and it was roomier in his three-car garage. My uncles looped the rope over the rafters in the ceiling to hoist the pig off the floor. I held my breath against the taut sound of rope rubbing against the I-beam, the creaking sound of the pig's spinning weight. Uncle Clemente kicked the large plastic pail under the limp carcass. His cigarette dangled from the corner of his lip, the ash longer than the cigarette. He picked up a bucket of boiling water, doused the pig, and stood back. It swayed in the air, encased in a swirl of steam. Both Uncle Clemente and Uncle David began to rasp its skin with a kind of flexible steel blade, looped and held together by a wooden handle. They worked like lumberjacks in a squatting dance, dragging the blades over the pig's haunches, down its round belly, and to its ears close to the floor. Taking turns ridding the pig of its fine hair. Uncle Clemente's glasses clouded as he worked in the putrid steam. My Uncle David then stepped in and held the pig to keep it from turning. My Uncle Clemente wiped his knife on his jeans, moved close, and leaned on the pig with one hand to steady its weight. He adjusted his footing, bent slightly before he wiped his glasses in little circles with his thumb. He looked up at me for a second before slashing the pig's throat with one swift swipe. I wanted to turn away but was drawn to the blood's first squirt as it gurgled and streamed into the plastic pail. It turned purple as it hit the bottom of the blue pail and then liters of it became red, almost black, once again. My Uncle Clemente looked at me and grinned. He always liked to tease.

My father saw me come out of the garage, looked up and smiled. He had been busy digging a large hole for the pig's guts beside the fig tree and between the rows of peppers. It was good fertilizer, he'd say. Without asking, I walked toward him and picked up a shovel to help. A daddy longlegs had been hiding under the handle and it waltzed up my arm. I let it crawl on the back of my hand before raising it safely to one of the branches above.

"What you do?" my father said. And almost as if catching himself, "You want to help?" He sat on his haunches and hung his head between his knees. I wanted to leave. My father was spending more and more time in the basement, entertaining friends in the middle of the day with his homemade wine and *presunto*. He was getting meaner with his words. My mother said that work would pick up soon; Portuguese people were doing better and could now afford to renovate their basements. They'd need his truck to help them remove all that soil.

His eyes remained fixed on me as I dropped the shovel.

"Here, come with me."

I followed him back into the garage. The first pail was now full and ready for the women who would boil it for hours with parsley, garlic, and rice until it turned black and thick like mud and was ready to be forced into the bleached intestines to make sausage. Tomorrow my mother would cut one up and mangle it in a frying pan with olive oil. We'd spread it across our toast, the day before and where it came from forgotten.

"*Pronto,* Clemente. I ready with the hole!"

My Uncle Clemente placed a large stainless steel pail under the pig. I could feel my father's hands on my shoulders; they were large and sun-dark, and their backs were covered with golden hair. My hands were small and fine and white, and the hair on them wasn't visible, just felt like peach fuzz. A gentle squeeze was my cue to look up, pay attention. My Uncle Clemente raised a long

knife over his head, turned to me and smiled once again
before he plunged the knife into the pig's belly, exposed
the inches of white fatty layers that opened like flowers in
time-lapse photography. He sliced firmly down to the
pig's gullet then stood back. Foul gases and steam puffed
from the bloated pig. My uncle turned around. His
Coke-bottle glasses had steamed over. Behind him the
intestines slowly tumbled out into the pail, all blue and
purple and milky as the pig swayed in suspension. With a
touch of ceremony, my father took a drink of wine and
passed it around to the men. They all drank and mumbled prayers of thanks as they made the sign of the cross.
The stench wafted across the garage and dug into our
hair and clothes and throats. My father offered me the
cup of wine but my stomach churned and my head spun.

"*Filho*, bring this stuff to the hole I dig outside." He
pointed to the jumble of guts. He stopped in mid-
sentence to watch me spew the few pieces of toast I'd had
that morning all over the garage floor. My Uncle David
rolled his eyes and Uncle Clemente just shook his head,
another thing to hose down on what was an already busy
day. My father came over and lifted me up. I tucked my
head and snotty nose into his collar, took in his scent of
Old Spice as we moved through the backyard then down
the stairs into the cool darkness of the basement. I could
see my mother in the cellar kitchen chopping onions.

"What happened?" she asked.

"He's no feeling good." My father cupped my face.
"Okay? . . . Okay?" He placed me on the covered sofa.
Everything in my uncle's basement—sofa, chairs, coffee
table, and the large wooden TV—had once been on the

main floor. The living room had been converted to a bedroom when my grandmother and Aunt Louisa came from Portugal. A large floral bedspread that hung from a line divided the basement kitchen and family room. It was held up by wooden clothes pegs with rusted hinges. When we had large family gatherings, the bedspread came down and was converted into a tablecloth for the large pieces of plywood sitting on A-frames that were used as a dining table. There was a strange sense of comfort in knowing the routines and in understanding the function of every object in the house.

My mother came to sit beside me in her wilted dress. Her hair was tucked under her kerchief. She gently stroked my hair. I closed my eyes and heard my father's footsteps as he moved away from me; her cool breath blew on my damp forehead. My aunts whispered behind the curtain. They sat around the kitchen table and chopped onions or parsley.

"It's been a few days now. Still not a word, not even close to finding him." I could hear my Aunt Louisa's frustration tugging at her voice.

"They took his name away, you know. They gave him a new name—*Shoeshine Boy,*" my Aunt Zelia replied. "This is not a Portuguese name."

"What that poor boy's mother must be feeling. She must be crying like a *Magdalena,* cursing the day she came here." There was only a moment of silent contemplation. "She knows, she must know, a mother knows."

"The news say he try saving money to buy a ticket for his mother, to go visit back home," Aunt Zelia added.

"I no hear that," Aunt Louisa interjected. "I hear

other stories about that boy and what boys like him shining shoes do for extra money."

My mother moved back into the smoky kitchen. The
discussion continued but no longer penetrated the
padded bedspread that divided our two worlds. My aunts
had taken note of my mother's admonitions.

It was hot. I needed air.

Quietly, I made my way upstairs and out the front
door and onto my bike. I took hungry gulps, filling my
lungs to clear my nose of the smell that attached itself
to me.

"Hey!"

I looked to Manny's veranda. All I could see was his
curly black hair above the porch railing. He ran to meet
me at the gate.

"Let's go!" I said.

"We can't."

I saw his mother at the front door calling him inside.
She sounded anxious and mad.

"They found him on a rooftop . . . Yonge Street . . .
a massage parlor . . . under some boards, drowned . . .
like garbage." Manny punched the words into the still
summer air. He shrugged his shoulders then, wide-eyed,
whispered, "He's dead."

I didn't need to ask *who* was dead.

"Mannelinho!" his mother wailed.

Manny jumped up all five steps of his porch and the
screen door slammed behind him as he disappeared into
his house.

Stunned, I pedaled my way home. I found myself in
our unfinished basement. The floor was concrete,

painted in battleship gray, and the walls were covered with wood-paneled wainscoting. It was an open space with exposed joists, and it was partitioned by function. At the far end was the laundry area with washing machine and double laundry tub; across from it was the stove— every self-respecting Portuguese had a kitchen in the basement. The rest of the basement had an old backseat of a Chevy my father brought home one day and a console television that stood next to the doorway to our *adega,* where the fat-bellied oak barrels rested on their wooden blocks. An old hospital sheet with three blue lines on it marked the entry to this spot.

I flicked on the TV and sat back on the seat, where the backs of my legs stuck to the leather. In a daze I rolled down my tube socks and scratched the itchy red ring that encircled my shins and calves. My socks had been held up all day long by elastic bands that my mother kept in a small bag in a drawer. I rubbed the groove that had been carved into my leg.

We didn't have cable, only CBC and, depending on the weather, channel 7, which was 79 on the second dial. Anita Bryant strolled through an orange grove in her shiny white dress and perfectly coiffed hair. She looked so different from the woman who was leading the Save Our Children campaign. "And remember, breakfast without orange juice is like a day without sunshine." I could feel my sister move behind the couch, and when I looked back I saw she had a towel wound like a genie's turban on her head.

"She should have stuck to selling oranges," my sister said.

The news resumed. My sister sat next to me and tucked her legs under her bum. I leaned into the TV.

"This is the street corner where Emanuel Jaques was last seen. Four days ago he was seen here shining shoes and then disappeared into what many consider the cesspool of the city, Yonge Street. Reports suggest that he and his brother and friend were approached by a man . . ."

Terri unwrapped the towel to scrunch up her wet hair and I could smell the Ivory soap.

"Emanuel's older brother alleges a man asked . . . thirty-five dollars." My mind began to wander. "He and his friend to move camera equipment . . . call home . . . to see . . . and upon his return, Emanuel was gone . . . vanished." They plastered a picture of the large-eyed boy on the screen. It was all we had seen the last few days. He had a soft face and his smile seemed sincere between the large curls that framed his cheeks. "The search is over. The body of a twelve-year-old boy police have identified as Emanuel Jaques has been found on the rooftop of—"

"Ouch!" I roared. My sister had pinched my thigh.

"Don't ever go with anyone. Got it?" She moved to turn off the television, but stopped when the hysteric wails of a mother trilled behind the interviewer's questions. She was speaking Portuguese. I understood the words, what she was saying, the pain and suffering in what could not be translated. It somehow felt too close to home.

I skidded my bike into my uncle's garage. There wasn't much left of the pig; only the hind legs remained to be cured as they dangled and twisted from the wooden rafters. The uncles had whittled away with their saws, and the pieces of meat had been divided: organ bucket, rib bucket, and so on. I was trying to catch my breath so I could tell them the news. I had dropped my bike on the gravel laneway, ignoring the kickstand. Before I could say anything, my Uncle Clemente caught me around the waist, laughed as he tried to shove something in my mouth. The men cheered him on as I squirmed in his hold. My uncle had rammed the pig's tail in my mouth. Part of it curled around my tongue and the rest lodged in the roof of my mouth. They all laughed as I gagged then spat it out. I stood hunched over, building saliva to spit the taste out of my mouth. They patted me on the back. I was caught off guard. I looked to my father.

"You is a man now," he whispered, his stubble scraping against my cheek.

I spat the taste out of my mouth, grabbed at my father's warm wine and threw it hard against the back of my throat. This led to another wave of "*Força!*" and further bouts of approval with "*Um homem.* A man now."

Everything became blurred by the tears that blanketed my eyeballs. The sounds around me became muted. I scanned the faces with their mouths wide open. I smeared the wine across my lips.

They don't know yet. They don't know about Emanuel.

I won't tell them.

I picked up my bike and sped away.

I will hold on to this, certain it will hurt them.

I rode past all those boarded-up shops on Queen Street, past all the drunks toward Spadina . . . *My lungs were filled with a burning fire. My throat was dry and their voices grew* nearer, louder: *"Treat you good, like one of the boys"* . . . City Hall and then Yonge Street . . . *I could hear the thunder of their feet on cement. They clipped my heels and I fell forward with my hands splayed out like spiders. My wrists buckled against the pavement. I looked at my hands, striped with thin lines like red hair* . . . I rode up the street, passed the neon signs and the dirty curbs that lined the new Eaton Centre . . . *They touched me with their strong hands. They tugged at my shirt, tore at me as I looked up into a searing sun, and they groped. I wanted to dip my hands into cold water to soothe their burning* . . . The haunting images left me as I pedaled faster and allowed the breeze to rush up my nose and fill my lungs.

I stopped just above Dundas Street—across the street from a place called Charlie's Angels that had been cordoned off with yellow tape. I stood there straddling my bike, leaning over my handlebars, and watched along with the news teams, reporters, and everyone else who gathered. Silence. We all seemed to be waiting for something. There were so many people around and yet I felt a reverence, a numbing quiet, alone in a big city I didn't recognize underneath a blood-orange sun.

I pedaled my way back home, slowly now, and turned up Palmerston Avenue. I don't know how long I had been away. Everyone should have been outside; the streetlights weren't on yet. *I'm sure they've heard by now.* I pedaled so slowly I was barely moving, fighting to keep my balance as I curved up the sidewalk, grappling the handlebars. *Where is everyone?* I passed one expectant porch after another where plastic crates held empty pop bottles, where rubber mats awaited muddy shoes, and where the blue-and-white glazed saints, *azulejos,* whispered empty blessings.

My mother moved toward me down the empty street. I could see the white lace of her slip, lit by the moonlight, peeking from the bottom of her dress. As she met me I cowered slightly. She smelled of blood sausages and onions and warm paprika.

"Where did you go? Get in that house, now!" There was fear and anger tinged with relief in her voice.

I walked my bike through our front gate and dropped it on the lawn. The wheel spun slowly in the air.

She drew her sweater tightly across her breasts, tucked her hands under her armpits and then shivered. It wasn't cold. Once inside I turned to see her look through the screen door before sliding the handle to LOCK. Then she closed the front door and did the same. It was the first time I heard the click of the deadbolt.

I lay in bed. The sound of the lock clicking played itself in my head only to be disturbed by the sudden clang of our garage door. Before I heard the familiar sound of his boots, the cadence of his steps climbing the stairs, there was always his smell: pig fat, Craven A cigarettes, and the sweetness of homemade wine. The same smell that would drift from laneways and garages, years later, to find me in my bed.

As he walked in I saw his face; it was shiny, pinkish-red like the skin underneath a scab. He sat by my bed with his face covered in droplets of sweat. He looked away for one moment and rocked forward as if he'd thought better of it and would leave.

I inhaled.

He sat back down again, looking out my open window. He turned to face me, opened his mouth to say something but stopped. I could see his tired eyes. He reached over and carefully brushed my hair from my forehead with his thick fingers. I didn't want him to cry.

"You not hurt?" He took another deep breath. He was about to say something else, but instead got up. "Close you light," he mumbled. Then he quietly shut the door behind him.

~ *SENHOR CANADA* ~

JULY 1, 1978

8:40 A.M. If I pressed my forehead against the mesh screen of my bedroom window, craned my neck and looked down at a certain angle, I could see my father on the veranda with his little straw hat, a Sam Sneed, perched on his head, his red-and-white striped shirt— short-sleeved, of course—and his plaid pants that the kids on the street jokingly called "all seasons," like the tires. His slippered feet balanced on the wrought-iron railing as he tied the flag to the pole. The tip of the flag swept against the edge of the bathtub, standing upright on one end to form an enameled alcove, the focal point of our garden. Jesus stood inside it, all two feet of him, clutching at his plump Sacred Heart amid the strewn plastic flowers. With the door and windows already open, my father moved to the living room, turned on the large console stereo—the kind that also contained a mirrored miniature bar behind a drop-leaf panel—and placed the single on the turntable. He set the volume to HIGH.

My mother had secretly stored her figurines safely in her linen drawer the night before, afraid they would scooch slowly along the vibrating furniture and smash onto her parquet floors. My sister had left before my father got up. She had arranged a sleepover with her friend Margaret. My mother would also be leaving; she "needed" to help her sister season the meat for *chouriço*.

There was the initial scratch and pop of the needle hitting vinyl because of his already unsteady hand. He appeared on the veranda, just in time.

> *O Canada!*
> *Our home and native land!*
> *True patriot love in all thy sons command.*

He stood there for the whole song, stiff and serious, his hand crossed over his heart. Then he sat in his folding chair with a Molson Ex in hand. It was quite a sight: the little man, his mismatched attire, wrapped in his adopted patriotism as the anthem blared from our windows and out our door onto Palmerston Avenue. It had become his annual Canada Day ritual—his alone.

My mother was in her room. "You'll be okay?" she yelled over the horns and tubas as she wrapped her kerchief around her head. I nodded then looked down at my bare feet; I hadn't even dressed yet. She lifted my chin gently with her index finger curled like a comma.

"Are you sure you want to stay? Maybe you want to come with me!" she shouted.

I reminded her that I was twelve—almost thirteen—and that I could take care of things. I was leaving, I tried to convince her, to go play at Manny's house. I gently guided her down the hall toward the kitchen and the sliding doors. She hesitated for a moment, looked over my shoulder to see my father leaning over the fence, tapping his feet from one side to the next. The blaring music was becoming too much already. She gnashed her teeth through a strained smile then shuffled her way out the back door, out through the garage. She decided to take the long route through the laneway. It was probably best.

My mother and sister would both be gone the whole day. I decided to stay upstairs in my room, looking at my digital clock with its orange numbers, willing the day to wilt away. I would arrange my Star Wars cards yet again—Chewbacca at the front of the deck, Princess Leia at the back. I was getting too old for them but in a strange way they comforted me, and I knew they'd be worth something one day. When I got bored I flipped open my sketch pad and drew objects in my room: a chair, the rumpled sheets on my bed. I tried a perspective drawing of my room that got smaller with every failed attempt.

The 45 was set on REPEAT. The arm of the turntable, with its taped penny for added weight, moved slowly to its rest position; denied its reprieve, it then jerked and swung back over the record and into the fine grooves.

. . . With glowing hearts we see thee rise,
The True North strong and free!

10:03 A.M. If the couple of years were any indication, he
would continue this way for the better part of the day
with few interruptions: to get another beer, a glass of
wine, or to shed an article of clothing in the growing July
heat. At one point that morning I ventured into the
kitchen to pour myself a glass of milk.

"What you do?"

He caught me off guard. The swinging fridge door
nudged my hand, which sent the bottle of milk to the
floor. It shattered. The milk spread across the linoleum,
pooled around his bare feet.

"I'll clean it up . . . watch your . . ."

He walked toward me.

"*Pai*, watch it!"

"You clean up this mess. I no want to live like pigs!"

I choked as he grabbed me by the collar and tried to
lift me off the floor to face him. When he couldn't, he
bent down instead. I didn't want to look; I didn't want
to see the redness in his round face or smell his morning breath mixed with beer. He had never hit me before
and he was proud of telling everyone, especially family,
that he had never found a reason to discipline his children like they did "back home"—like dogs, he'd say. I
felt his gnarled fingers slowly let go. He patted the back
of my T-shirt flat.

"You is good boy. I no hurt you. I no want you to cut
you feet, that's all." The lines in the corners of his eyes

bunched up like those accordion fans we made with paper.

I reached down to grab the pieces of broken glass. He left the kitchen with a cold beer and I followed the trail of small red dots that his right foot stamped across the hallway floor.

11:14 A.M. A canvasing politician arrived just before lunch.

"Hello, Mr. . . ."—he looked at his clipboard—"Rebelo? You're a fine Canadian to honor your country this way."

"Yes, I Canadian."

"Well, the arrogance of this government." He shook his head for effect. "This prime minister is destroying—"

"Who?"

"Mr. Trudeau is destroying the very fabric of—"

"Out!" my father hollered. He shouted it again, louder, so that he could be heard over the anthem. "Out! Get-out-a-here!" My father strained his neck and gestured a kick, the same way he was taught to kick a football—with the inside of his foot, toes pointing outward.

"I don't quite understand—" the politician squirmed.

"I come from Portugal twenty-three-ago-years." His thick accent was made thicker by his drunken slur. "I come to Canada with no cash-money—my feet is my shoes! My hands, they hard!" He pounded his chest; I heard the muffled hollowness. "Trudeau is the man. He promise to make things easy for bring my family over here. He keep his promise."

The ever-smiling politician slowly made his way out, closing the gate behind him.

> . . . and stand on guard,
> O Canada, we stand on guard for thee.

My father's angry voice melded with the anthem, became one as the words spread across our tiny manicured lawn to chase down the retreating politician and his assistant.

12:10 P.M. Mr. Grayson said that if I am serious about becoming an artist I should sketch everything, even the most mundane things. I could sit behind the aquarium in my room for hours, drawing it. It was filled with guppies, the fancy-tailed variety: Leopard and Sunburst. A boxed kaleidoscope. The fake background bought at the pet store by the foot had been precisely measured and taped to the back of the aquarium, an underwater forest of greens and swirling browns. My father bought a bag of red gravel and a bag of white. I remember when he rinsed it and mixed the colors together.

"Like Canada flag," he said.

"I wanted natural," I mumbled.

He hadn't heard me. My father had also purchased a plastic figure to place at the bottom of the aquarium. It was an old-fashioned deep-sea diver with one of those metal globe helmets. He would try to open the treasure chest filled to the brim with pearls and jewels, but every ten seconds or so a few bubbles would erupt from his golden mask and wobble to the surface along with the diver, who would then be jolted by the hose that connected his helmet to the base. The lid of the treasure chest would close again, covering the elusive riches inside. The diver would then sink back down. He kept trying to pry it open, always with the same result. I don't know why I found this so fascinating. What was it that kept me glued to his failed attempts?

> *. . . O Canada, glorious and free!*
> *We stand on guard for thee.*

1:43 P.M. It was getting harder for him to stand for the anthem. He struggled with the arms of his chair and the wrought-iron railing before settling back. He hadn't eaten a thing. He was wearing only his hat and stained boxer shorts. I was embarrassed by his farmer's tan; his white feet and pasty torso were clearly lined where his socks and sleeves ended. I sat, trapped like a caged bird, hoping he would come inside and fall asleep so I could turn off the music and get outside. I'd hop on my bike and ride past Robinson and onto Bathurst Street, farther and farther toward the island airport and away from my house.

"*Pai*, come inside," I pleaded through the screen door. "*Pai!*"—a little louder this time—"I'll make you lunch. Come inside."

He turned and looked at me, his head bobbing.

"I coming," he slurred, his eyelids weighted.

He didn't move. I opened the screen door and helped him get up. I saw my friend Agnes's mother, Senhora Gloria, dressed in her customary brown habit, open Mr.

Pinto's gate across the street. She looked right at us as she closed it behind her, smiled and raised her hand halfway. I looked away just as my father reached for my hand and stumbled over the threshold. I quickly shut the door and turned the lock.

He took three bites of his tuna sandwich in front of the TV before he was out cold. In the kitchen, I collected all the empties and placed them back in the box. I washed the patch of floor still sticky from this morning. When I was certain he was asleep, I turned off the TV and went into the living room to lower the stereo, aware that turning it off completely might rouse him.

Back in my room I could see Senhora Gloria making her rounds across the street, knocking on doors and asking for more money for the church. She would move up Palmerston all the way to College Street and then work her way back on the other side of the road, our side. I was in love with her daughter Agnes, who said her mother wasn't a nun but when she got dressed to do the work of the Lord she would always begin by reciting a novena of indulgence, so that her sins could be forgiven.

"My brother isn't really my brother," Agnes had said.

I didn't answer.

"My mother had another husband but he hit her so she left him." I didn't really know what that meant; I didn't think Portuguese people were allowed to "leave."

2:38 P.M. The second-floor kitchen window opened onto the gently sloped roof below. I wedged the plunger in the window jam and unfurled the beach towel my sister kept next to the sill; the baby oil and transistor radio remained on the floor. I screened my eyes against the sun and hopped quickly onto the towel; the soles of my feet were seared by the shingled roof.

I knew my friends and other boys from the neighborhood would stop at our laneway on their bikes, where they'd get a clear view of my sister tanning in her bikini. Some would even venture a holler and something rude about her tits or her ass. Without missing a beat, her toe tapping, her arm would shoot up and she'd give them the middle finger. I wanted to say something, to defend her honor, but could never build up the nerve.

I lay back and tucked my hands behind my head. The pole that held the sagging line of white sheets and underwear creaked with every puff of wind. I wanted to escape—saw how easy it would be to throw myself onto the pole and slide down, my inner thighs burning on the hot metal, crash into the cool patch of kale in the garden. I could run to the garage, feel for the latch on the door and roll it up, flood it with light and air and dust. I could jump on my bike, ride up the alley, and venture farther than ever to an undiscovered park or an alley unturned—run down the clock.

I could let him wake up alone.

3:14 P.M

> . . . With glowing hearts we see thee rise,
> The True North strong and free!

~ *169* ~

The anthem blared once again. I crawled through the window and ran toward my bedroom, the floating blobs in my eyes adjusting to the light. I looked out my bedroom window. He must have run out of beer; he held a glass of homemade wine and stretched his arms into the hazy air. A full jug of wine, his reserve, sat tucked under his lawn chair. I caught a glimpse of Senhora Gloria as she came down the road toward our house. I watched her get closer and then I closed my eyes and willed her to continue down the road, skip our house altogether. When I opened my eyes she was undoing the latch to our wrought-iron gate. My father, half dressed, made his way down to the garden and bent over to wipe Jesus' face with his hairy forearm. I worried that if he squatted too low he would topple into his shrine.

"Ah . . . Senhor Manuel. You make a party?" She nodded her approval. People knew they were expected to speak to him in English—*You live in Canada now,* is what he'd say.

"You no hot . . . in that Jesus dress?"

"God keep me fresh, Senhor Manuel."

"Me too." He turned to point at the glass of red wine that teetered on top of the curved alcove. She pretended not to notice. I could tell that she was trying very hard not to look at his groin.

"Well . . . I come and ask you." She sensed the need to be delicate. "You is a good man. This country is good. Now is time to give to church."

"Why?" He waited for an answer. There was none. "The church no give me nothing."

"*Uma pia batismal*—we need new one and we ask the *communidade* to—"

"For what?" He moved directly in front of her like a bully. "For you to wash youself between the legs, you *pinta* smell fresh for you to make sex with Padre Costa?"

He grinned, pleased with himself.

She froze. Red shot through her face. She turned; her robe of brown swirled with her, then kicked back against her calves as she quickly retreated down the street.

He looked up at me and laughed aloud. I hated him, and I hated myself for needing to stay.

I moved away from the window and returned to my bench in front of the aquarium. The water rippled with the vibrations of the anthem. If I tried hard I could forget almost anything just by looking at my deep-sea diver and the fish. The male guppies were in constant competition. They darted in one direction or crossed over the front trying to stop the female guppies, corner them, before they tilted their penises sideways as they rubbed against the females and tried to stick them in. The males were the colorful ones; the females were plain and gray. A few of the females were pregnant; you could tell by their black abdomens, that's what the chapter "Breeding Guppies" said.

One of the large females swam quickly to the surface, took in a gulp of air, then stopped. She began to drop her "fry," the little babies that have eyes bigger than their bodies. The other fish shot into a frenzy. Many gobbled up the babies as they plopped out of their mother. Even she got a few herself, took them in whole. Some males saw this as a perfect opportunity to have sex. I tried to tap on the glass, to stop them from eating, but then sat back helplessly to watch.

> *. . . and stand on guard,*
> *O Canada, we stand on guard for thee.*

5:08 P.M I thought it was best to bring him inside so he could watch the news read by his favorite anchor, Tom Gibney. My mother would be home soon. As I came down the stairs I didn't even notice the anthem. I touched the mesh of the screen door. His slightly parted lips meant he was sleeping.

"*Pai!*" I scratched the screen.

"*Pai!* The news is on." He stirred. I opened the door slightly to step out. That's when I saw the caravan of bikes meandering down our street. I let the screen door slam and retreated to my room.

I must have woken him, because I soon heard him shouting out the names of my friends. They were beginning to gather around our home on their bikes, expectantly. It was time for this year's races. This, too, had become part of the Canada Day celebration.

"Boys!" he yelled. "Come here!"

This was the pre-race ritual; they had to introduce themselves formally. They usually giggled through this part. He would then have them place their hands over their hearts like Americans and sing the national anthem. There they were, mirroring the statue of Jesus, holding on to their hearts. They never asked for me. Tomorrow, they would pretend nothing had happened, wouldn't mention a thing.

Once the opening exercises were finished they raced around the block and through the laneways. The winner was always rewarded with a dollar. My father had made a special trip to the bank, only the day before, to change a twenty into ones. Off they went—Manny on his banana seat with its forked front, Dennis on his new Chopper, and a few of the younger boys on their bikes: George, Carlos, and Steven. They pedaled up the street until they disappeared around the corner. Ten minutes later my father walked down the path to the front gate, wearing only his yellowed boxer shorts and his little straw hat. His face, shoulders, and back were as red as a steamed lobster. He greeted the winner and awarded the prize with such excitement that it was difficult for him to stand. Every so often he fell and the boys would laugh. He would then crawl up the stairs and onto the veranda.

"On your marks, go!" And they were off again. He staggered back to his chair. I looked away, shrouded myself behind the sheer curtains. I waited for the cheers and screams of the returning boys before I took a quick look to see who had won.

Over and over again, the same scene played itself out. I tried hard to push it all away, but it drove me crazy to have him down there, laughed at by my friends. I sat by my aquarium watching the guppies dart, mesmerized by the determined stupidity of the deep-sea diver. I sat on my bed counting my cards. I thought of Agnes and then her mother, Senhora Gloria. I tried to think of other things, like the orphan kids from Africa on those sponsorship commercials; they always had those big bellies and they never bothered to shoo the flies away from their noses and lips. That usually made the sexual urges disappear.

If I pressed my ear right up to the mesh screen of my bedroom window I could hear the city. The air, punctuated by the sounds of sirens, ambulances and fire trucks, smelled thick and warm. I wanted to meet these noises and return to spread exaggerated tales of blood and smoke and dead people being carried away on stretchers.

O Canada!
Our home and native land!
True patriot love in all thy sons command.

6:51 P.M They wouldn't leave. My father had bestowed his final dollar prize on Manny, but they wanted more. Manny looked up at my window to see if I was there, but I was careful to hide out of sight. I could hear them jeering and pestering my father. They laughed as he stumbled off the path and onto the lawn. I saw their faces grow bolder, angrier.

"You fucken drunk!" Manny shouted.

"Get-out-a-yere!" my father yelled.

"He's embarrassed of you." Manny looked up again to my window. "Afraid to hang around us anymore cause you're a drunk."

"Get out!"

They all continued to laugh except for Manny. The others rattled our fence. There was a moment when I wanted to throw myself out the window, imagined I could land softly on my feet and they would scurry in fear. My legs felt wobbly and my head began to throb and hurt; the kind of pain you get from taking water up your nose in the pool, that sort of brain-freezing pain, the kind you're helpless to stop. Manny then kicked the wrought-iron fence; all the while he looked up at my window. I could see my father. He managed to get up and moved toward the garden hose. He fumbled with the nozzle then turned on the water. As my father moved toward the boys, some scooted off, but others, like Manny and Dennis, sat solidly on their bikes, defiant. It was as if they welcomed the cold water on such a hot day. As he moved onto the veranda his feet became tangled in the loops of the hose. He lost his footing and fell backward, silently tumbled down the green-turfed steps and landed facedown on the Interlock path. His body opened up for a moment and then pulled tightly into a ball, like a pill bug, still.

As he slowly raised his head I could see the horror on their faces. Everyone took off, scattered nervously.

I waited.

He wasn't getting up.

The hose danced like a spitting cobra without its charmer. The water cut great curves and arches against the sky. The nozzle finally wedged itself in a curlicue of the wrought iron, where it sprayed against the flag, which flapped like a drenched towel.

He still wasn't up.

I ran downstairs, looked out the storm door to make sure that no one was around, then leapt down the veranda stairs in one bound. He lay contorted, beads of sweat gleaming as they trickled down his bald head. The blood that ran from his nose covered his lips like a clown's.

"*Pai! Acorda!* Wake up!" I wedged my arms under his armpits, dragged him step by step into our house. In his room I hoisted him onto the bed as he clutched his invisible heart, silently mouthing the words to the anthem. But the tempo was lost; he was a man alone with his words. He caught me with his steel-blue gaze, his eyes darted around my face before they slowed down, locked with mine. I kept thinking about how big his head was compared to the rest of his shriveled little body.

"*Não quero mais sonhos.*" His voice strained then cracked. "Dreams, no more dreams." His eyes were big. "You the man! You my little man." He turned to his side and through the snorting sobs came, "*Sonhos, não quero mais sonhos,*" until the words trailed off into a whisper.

7:36 P.M I walked outside, turned off the hose, and cleared the drenched veranda of everything: clothing, beer bottles, his vinyl chair. I placed his hat on my head. I stopped to look at Jesus standing there with his smug expression, his feet covered in gaudy pink and blue plastic flowers. I walked into the house and dropped everything on the living room floor, shut all the windows and locked the front door before I moved to turn off the stereo. My eyes became fixed on the wobbling record. I changed the record speed to SLOW. The voice became long and distant, a song buried in a dark tunnel as it struggled to find its way out. I was getting used to hearing and seeing things in that way. The needle settled in a groove, caught: *t . . . h . . . e . . . r . . . i . . . s . . . e—t . . . h . . . e . . . r . . . i . . . s . . . e—t . . . h . . . e . . . r . . . i . . . s . . . e—t . . . h . . . e . . . r . . . i . . . s . . . e . . .*

~ POUNDING THEIR SHADOWS ~

WHEN I WAS ALONE, WHEN my friends didn't walk home from school with me or I managed to dodge into a laneway, there was something special about the glimmer of a silvery bit of metal buried underneath gravel and dead leaves or the burnt red of a rusted iron rod. I was fifteen and although it wasn't expected of me anymore, I still found myself picking up small shards of metal or flattened tin cans. The real prize was "in the orange," as I liked to call it, a thin sheet of copper or a ball of knotted copper wire.

Like the clicking sounds of old telegraph machines that sliced through the wind on sagging wires, Mother's words rang clear: *Listen to the wind; see the wind.* I would raise a moistened finger or toss a blade of grass into the air to gauge where pieces of corrugated roof may have blown or tin cans rolled into the narrow gullies between garages.

These scraps were my mother's treasures, and I was glad to offer them to her.

Much of what I found had gathered in the narrow crawl space, probably a foot at its widest point, that separated our garage from my father's pigeon house. When I was a boy I loved to play in the aviary and sit on a small stool in the corner with my drawing pencils and paper. I loved the way the pigeons' wings fluttered as they flew short distances from perch to perch, how their puffed breasts squeezed into the smallish holes, how they sidestepped on the narrow ledges my father had fixed to the wall. I especially loved the whistle in their wings, whirring in my ears as their soft plumes see-sawed all the way down to the encrusted ground. It was their flight that I tried to record in my drawing book, the mad frenzy of beating wings in the light that filtered through a Plexiglas roof and penetrated the dried pigeon shit like a stained glass window.

I came in through the garage and peered through the chicken-wire frame of the aviary. There was nothing inside. It had been empty for a few years. I allowed myself to remember how gentle my father had been when he would nudge a pigeon's breast up with his knuckles. The pigeon would peck at his fist. But his hand would always be rewarded with one or two small eggs that nestled in the webbing between his fingers, or a hatchling, its bulging eyes and stiff white feathers bursting from its pimply raw skin.

"Just one drop each, *filho*," he would say.

I would hover the dropper over their greedy beaks, pinch the end and allow the droplet to bulge at the tip before it fell into their pink gullets.

I ran down the path and made my way up to the attic. I tipped my knapsack over, spilling the contents across my mother's workspace, an old Singer sewing machine that hung upside down. She looked at my "catch of the day" and her eyes narrowed with the clear idea of where the key to the Spam can or that spring would go. She made me feel like it was all destined, as if there was importance in my work, and that together something wonderful was possible.

"Ahhh, and look at this cup." She rolled the child's tin cup between her palms. "A hat! It would make a wonderful fisherman's hat."

She held it above the seated figure she was working on, a man about a foot high with a cable-knit sweater she had carefully painted. The cup sat nicely proportioned to his head.

"*My* fisherman," she nodded. She searched in my expression for a shared recognition of who this latest whirligig figure was. I pretended to know and it gave her such satisfaction. She allowed me to sit with her in the attic. Quietly, against the glow of candlelight, her shredded hands betrayed how gingerly she worked the metal, holding the tin snips with such confidence and power.

"Do your hands hurt?" I asked.

"Sometimes," she paused to lift her head and stretch her neck. The faint smoke caused by the soldering drifted upward in curvy streaks. "But it's a good hurt."

"*Mãe*, there's no such thing."

"Oh, but there is, *filho*."

I heard my father's muffled curses; he was sure to be drunk by now, submersed in the basement like a mole, drinking from his store of homemade wine.

"When your father brought me here," she began her story without disrupting the flow of her work, "the first thing I saw on that pier in Halifax was a weathervane, a green rooster with four cups that caught the wind and spun in the ocean air. It reminded me of home, the place I wanted to leave and the people I missed already."

My father continued to swear at the top of his lungs. I could place exactly where he was by how loud he was—the top of the basement stairs. My mother searched on her table for the tin snips, desperately looking for something to drown him out.

My mother spent most of her time in the attic, twisting and hammering away at her scraps of metal. My sister was hardly ever at home; she seemed to always be studying for something. I had constructed my own set of rules for friends, how they were not to call on me or drop by without arranging things beforehand. I was angry that I allowed him to penetrate my world the way he did, but I thought it would be easier.

A few months earlier my Aunt Louisa had convinced my mother to visit Paulo, a faith healer from Brazil who claimed to heal sickness by ridding people like my father of the evil spirits that inhabited them.

"What else is there to do?" Aunt Louisa had said.

I could hear their voices through the heating vent in my room. I rolled the slatted grate wider.

"I'm not sure, Louisa. I don't like this man everyone is talking about."

"It can't hurt. What is it that worries you?"

"Is he a man of God?"

"I can't answer that. But he's a man who might be

able to help. You've tried everything and still—" A sudden blast of hot air shot through the tunnel of galvanized metal and drowned out their voices.

My mother had gone to meet this healer and, a couple of hundred dollars later, returned with a bag of herbs that she would pinch like cotton candy and place in her cast iron skillet. I had seen her do this many times before, her solitary ritual. It was always performed when my father was out of the house. A match was dropped on the small mound of tumbled herbs; they would burn quickly into orange embers. Like incense, it was only when the glow left the charred twigs that the smoke would swirl in wisps. She'd sway the pan in front of her, walk into every room and say something, always mumbled. It had frightened me at first but then it became normal, like all things repeated.

The herbs were also versatile. To ensure their success even further, my mother had sewn tiny satchels no bigger than a dime and stuffed them with her herbs. She offered mine on a safety pin and fastened it on the strap of my undershirt. My sister didn't want one at first, afraid it would damage her clothes, but then, boldly in front of me, pinned it to the front clasp of her Dici bra. My mother had cuffed her ear lightly.

"What's the big deal?" my sister asked.

Embarrassed, I had left the room.

The herbs could also be boiled and the tea mixed with cod liver oil, which never really mixed, just congealed into a blob at the bottom of the small glass my mother offered us. My sister and I would pinch our noses then chase it down with milk.

My mother was willing to try anything. "That's the source," my Aunt Louisa had said one evening, pointing to the plant shelf filled with cacti, "the devil's plant!" Her eyes widened for greater effect and the raised mole on her forehead seemed to flash like a beacon. I had laughed. "You no mess with the devil," she trembled, "he lives in the best houses." She seemed pleased with herself for discovering the root of our troubles and for deadening my laughter. The next day, all the cacti were thrown out.

A snap in the wind brought my mother to attention. My father was silent for the time being. She looked out the attic window.

"Go to bed now, *filho*. Be quiet on your way down."

"Why don't you leave him, *Mãe*?" I asked.

Her chin lowered to her chest. She was growing weary of the question in its various forms.

"He needs me," she replied.

"Aren't you coming to bed?"

"No. There are still his boots to paint, baskets of fish to fill, and then I have to fix this small fan propeller I found last week." She patted the table with her hands in search of the propeller.

"Good night, *Mãe*." I was too old to kiss her.

I lay in bed thinking about my mother, her determination to make something out of nothing.

I thought about The Dream—why they came here. I always thought it had been for the same reason. Mother had her attic and her metal and us. But my father didn't seem to have anything; he didn't seem to want anything, as if The Dream wasn't worth holding on to. He dwelled on the "nothing." Still, she always protected him as if she needed to, had to. "We all have our crosses to bear," she'd say. "Remember. Despite it all, he's a good man. Just lost his way, I think."

I couldn't remember the last time I had gone to bed before midnight. Usually, the poisonous slurs that erupted from my father's mouth as he stood at the bottom of the stairs kept me from sleep. My sister, Terri, slept in the room next to me and at nineteen had honed a boldness that both excited and frightened me.

"Shhh!" was followed by, "Be quiet!" through her door.

One night it had the desired effect; he heard her and shuffled down the hallway. I could hear his hands sliding along the paneling in the corridor to guide him. He descended into the damp basement, grumbling, "*Putas* in my house." He was yelling those angry words, *cocksuckersh* and *fuckersh*—the *sh* sound was a trademark of our anglicized Portuguese. I wanted him to be like one of my uncles who got drunk and laughed, lay on a couch somewhere when no one was looking and slept it off. My father was different.

"Are you still up?" I hadn't heard my mother come into my room. She sat on my bed and tilted her head as if sorry for everything, as if it was her fault.

"Ma, he's driving me crazy!" My sister charged into my room. I sat up.

"He's going to bed soon, *paciência filha.*" My mother patted the edge of my bed, an invitation for her to come and lie down with us.

"*Putas!* Get out a here! This is my house! I no want fuckersh *putas* in my house!"

My mother instinctually drew my sister close to her. My blood raced as I saw Terri turn and, with exaggerated steps, as if to announce she was approaching, stomp down the stairs and through the long corridor. My mother raised her hand to her forehead and sighed deeply before hanging her head low. We waited.

"I want to sleep!" my sister yelled.

"This is my house!" he replied.

"Just go to bed and shut up, for God's sake, just shut the fuck up!"

My stomach hit my throat.

"And it's not *fuckersh*. There's no *shhh* in that fucken word. You've been in Canada all these years and—"

"I Canadian!" I could imagine him puffing out his chest and pounding it hard.

"You're a fucken pork chop! That's what they call us dad . . . pork chops!"

My mother sprang from my bed and ran down the stairs. A heat pricked at my brain as I followed. My sister had spat the words out like darts. I was glad she had said them, and I hoped the words had made him topple or cower in a corner.

Instead, my father stood in the kitchen with drenched boxers hanging on his frail body. His blotched face and head bobbed on his pasty torso. His eyelids were half closed and he tried to steady himself along the counter as my mother caught hold of my sister's shoulders, pulled her back, urged her to return to her room. I felt the guilt of wanting my sister to finish what she had begun.

My father knocked over the porcelain soap dish that sat next to the sink, and the swell of tension was broken by its smashing on the floor. My mother let go and I saw the flash of concern in my sister as she crouched down to pick up the pieces before his long white feet stepped on anything. It is what I would have done and I wanted her to stop. I wanted him to walk over the broken glass, to have the jagged pieces dig into the soles of his feet. My father bent over and grabbed her fisted hand in his and pulled her up until she stood next to him. I could see his white knuckled hand over hers. A trickle of blood appeared on the inside of her wrist, then made its way down her arm in a crooked line.

He let go. Slowly, my sister unfurled her fingers—opened her hand flat. A small piece of the soap dish lay buried in her palm. She picked the shard out of her hand and the blood spilled from the font. She closed her hand into a fist again.

"Get out! You no good, *puta.*"

"Terri, let's go to bed," I said.

She didn't hear me. She looked at my father, who seemed incapable of understanding what he had done. Her petite frame stood facing him. Something inside my sister took over. She lunged at my father and pushed him to the floor. She kicked him with her bare feet, first his chest, then his bald head.

He lay there, curled in the fetal position, absorbing each blow, helpless. My sister's rage had made her oblivious to the shards of china that lay scattered about, and she continued to pound his frame. Her bare feet slid through pee—I don't know if it was hers or his. She wobbled for only a second, regained her balance, and before she could continue her assault my mother caught her arms and tried to hold her back. The floor was covered in bloody scuff marks. She tried to tear herself from my mother's hold. I grabbed one of her wild legs, but she overpowered us, or we let her. Perhaps every blow to the head, every kick to his shins was *ours*.

Then Terri just stopped.

I lowered my eyes and turned sideways to allow her to pass. She left, as if all she had come down for was a glass of water. She exited into the dim corridor on her way back to bed; my mother followed behind.

I stayed to clean up the mess. I tried not to look at him lying there; his breath gurgled and rasped when he inhaled. He attempted to lift himself into a sitting position and look around the kitchen. One eye was swollen shut and there was blood smeared across his puffy cheeks. He saw me and raised his head, an invitation to help him. I didn't move. Only last week, at two o'clock in the morning, I had had to collect him from Wanda's front garden, up our street. He was completely naked in the cold night, peeing, her dog Poncho barking madly in the yard, snapping at the arc of urine. He hadn't asked for help then. Tonight he did. I bent down and threw his arm around my shoulder and dragged his clammy body to bed. As I tucked him in I saw my mother's silhouette move past the bedroom door, heard the click of the basement lights.

I followed her shadow into the wine cellar. My mother straddled one of the large oak barrels that sat in its wedged wooden bracket. She hung on to a leg of cured ham that dangled from the basement rafter, as she struggled to open the sliding window. The fresh autumn air poured into the room. She bent over the face of the barrel and plucked the cork free. The unfermented wine growled deep within its oaken belly before sputtering and spewing in a steady stream across the concrete floor. Barefooted, she moved to the next barrel and struggled to pull that cork out. And again, till all four barrels emptied themselves in rhythmic gulps.

She stood in her cotton nightgown that always smelled of sweet talcum powder. Her figure, with its maroon-stained hem, moved toward me. She took my hands then swung her shoulders in an invitation to dance. We danced through the streams of ruby red, splattering each other, twirling and spinning. My feet began to stick and I grew dizzy with her laughter.

"Stop, *Mãe* . . . I said stop!"

She had shut herself off from my voice but sensed my reluctance as I slowed down. Lacking a willing partner, she dropped my hands. She danced and twirled a few times more in a solitary and unconvincing flourish. For a moment she looked uncertain of where she was. She squatted over the puddle of wine and covered her face with her hands. There she sat, where the four streams of wine met, in the sweet smell of grape juice, amid the sounds of her sobs and the thin trickle dropping down the drainage hole.

"Go to bed now, *filho*." She swept her forearm across her face, moving the wisps of hair that stuck to her glowing forehead. "To bed, *filho*. I'll clean up."

Usually, on a Saturday morning I awoke to the smell of Lemon Pledge paste and the steady hum of my mother buffing the kitchen floor. This morning the house was silent. I faintly remember my mother peeking into my room; she used words like *hospital* and *stitches*. On my way down to the kitchen I thought I was alone, but saw my father's lump under the covers of his bed.

I grabbed a Joe Louis from the pantry and headed to the basement. *How had she left things?* The concrete floor was spotless, scoured and bleached. The stoppers had been placed back in the now hollow barrels. Only the sweet smell of unfermented wine lingered. The frosted window remained open. I climbed on top of a barrel and breathed in cold blowing wind that seared my lungs, then shut the window.

My father barely got out of bed that day. He left his room to pee or to pour himself a glass of milk mixed with a raw egg. I'm sure he thought that might cure what ailed him, his sore head and bruised back. The events of the previous evening were forgotten. I knew this because he had forced a painful smile when we met in the hallway and asked, "Where's your mother?" through a yawn.

I went to bed early, five o'clock. I made a sort of ritual of the event. I threw my flannel pajamas in the oven at two hundred degrees for only a couple of minutes, then quickly jumped into them and ran up to my bed and under my covers. I was fifteen and it was the sort of thing my mother used to do for us every Saturday night after our weekly baths. Usually, I'd be embarrassed, catching myself smiling with the warmth and pure joy that enveloped me. Tonight the joy was missing.

I was content to just sleep, but that eluded me also. I could hear my mother come up the stairs and move around the house. She entered my room then left, a trail of herbal smoke swirling after her.

I waited until I knew she had covered the whole house with her burnt offering, then followed her upstairs to the attic. She hunched over her workspace, her knees cramped next to the iron sewing machine that hung under the table. Aware of my presence, she motioned with her elbow to take a seat on the old chair that was once my grandmother Theresa's. I had found my mother on many a morning sleeping in this very chair. There had been a time when I felt I could swim in it. Now, I could barely cross my legs, the adult way—a habit I had only recently forced myself to pick up. I sat with my knees curled under my chin.

On the windowsill sat the fisherman my mother had been working on, his little tin hat tilted on the side of his head, his arms dangling over the edge of the small boat with *Avé* painted on its side. He held on to a long wire of dangling fish made from the simple twist of pop can tabs. Beside him, leaning against the windowpane, the blue-eyed boy seemed eager to ride his bicycle. The knees of his thinly wired legs would move with the slightest breath of air. My mother had made other whirligigs before; they were scattered across our vegetable garden, different colored birds whose wings turned freely on a simple rod, their beaks pointing into the wind.

"God sees everything," she said.

"How do you know?" I challenged. She stopped painting a dress on a small cutout of a girl, whose only completed feature was her hair.

"The wind tells me so," she said, "and time."

She turned to continue painting. God had loomed over our home and in our neighborhood; our lives and culture were controlled by what He represented, and I had believed.

On Monday my mother left early for work. I was home alone with my father, who hadn't worked in nine months. He had lost his license for driving drunk. He had been dumping some clean fill at the Leslie Spit and had almost run his dump truck into the lake. According to the police officer, when they towed the truck back onto the road, he lay in the front seat snoring, the cab filled to his waist with lake water.

I scrambled to get ready for school, but the sounds that came from his room frightened me. He was pleading with someone. Reluctantly, I stepped into his room and crept up beside him. He was huddled in his sheets, shaking uncontrollably.

He turned to face me, his eyes now bruised; his cut lip was healing, a dark scab had slowly formed. His head was dotted with small beads of sweat. His teeth rattled. His cool blue eyes darted across my face, searching for something recognizable. I could smell stale pee in his damp sheets, and when he opened his mouth traces of metal and sulfur rose from deep inside him. He grasped my arm, dug his nails in.

"She want to kill me . . . the black lady has a knife, *filho*. Run! Call the police. She want to kill me." He covered his head with the sheets and howled the same warnings from beneath his pillow.

"There's no one here."

"You fucken crazy. You kill me, you sonofabitch." Every muscle in his neck strained, his eyes bulged out of their sockets as his body squirmed in awkward spasms.

I ran to the phone in the hallway. *What happens in this house, stays in this house.* I dialed my mother at St. Michael's Hospital, and at the first ring placed the receiver back in its cradle. His groans boomed through the corridor. I lifted the receiver again, the blood swooshing across my ears, and dialed.

"Hello—" I paused for only a second. "I need an ambulance—55 Palmerston Avenue . . . It's my father . . . My name is Antonio . . . his son."

I sat on the chair beside the telephone in the hallway. They said they'd take him to Toronto Western. I could hear their exchanges, caught words like *hallucinations, stink, withdrawal, alcoholic.* Things were happening so fast.

"*Filho,* no let me go. They killing me, *filho.*"

They tucked the sheets taut under him, his arms stiff by his sides, and strapped him down with leather belts before wheeling him outside.

"Would you like to ride in the ambulance with us?"

"No," I said. I didn't want the neighbors to see me.

"They had no room for him in the hospital. They moved him. These are his blankets. Bring them to your father, *filho.*" A stuffed knapsack lay in the corner of the entrance hallway. Before I could say anything, she handed me an address—16 Ossington Avenue—clearly printed on a torn piece of paper. She kissed my forehead and opened the door for me.

"I'll take my bike."

It was mid-November and the air was beginning to sting. I pedaled my ten-speed along Queen Street, careful to avoid the streetcar tracks and sewer grates. I sped by Trinity Bellwoods Park and then the Candy Factory before crossing Shaw and the ominous gloom of the mental hospital. *Is this where he was? They said they'd be taking him to the hospital, Toronto Western.* I stopped and unraveled the piece of paper crushed between my hand and the handlebar. I moved toward Ossington Avenue then turned north, relieved I wouldn't have to go into the mental hospital. I came to a large blue door that matched the address on the paper. I knocked and a voice came through an intercom grate.

"I . . . I'm here to give something to my . . . Manuel."

The door opened with a buzz and I entered a dimly lit space; a mismatch of sofas and chairs with a large console television at the far end, its grainy glare washing over the furniture. A sign hung on the wall behind a counter: TORONTO WEST DETOX CENTRE. A large black man came around the counter and took the bag.

"Your father's there."

How does he know I'm his son, I thought. He pointed to a reclining chair wedged between two larger sofas. A small figure sat alone. I could see they were all watching Monday Night at the Movies—*Charly.* I approached slowly. *They're drunks,* I thought; the kind I saw on the street with their long beards and tattered clothes who laughed and smoked and drank Aqua Velva while others slept over heating vents or panhandled in store doorways. With every step toward my father the smell of stale cigarettes pushed against my nostrils. *He should be in a hospital . . . not here with these drunks.* A toothless woman came toward me and the black man at the door redirected her gently back to the sofa.

"You can't stay," he said in a surprisingly soft voice.

My father turned and saw me take some reluctant steps toward him. Before I reached him, he tried to get up; his knees buckled and a violent trembling began. He reached for my wrist.

"*Filho. Meu filho.* I so cold. They no turn on the heat. I ask and I ask but no one listen to me. Take me home. *Casa. Eu quero ir para a nossa casa.*"

I couldn't remember the last time he had spoken to me in Portuguese. He sounded so vulnerable when he uttered the phrase, the words strung together. He looked so helpless and lost, not the man I remembered as a boy. Tom—that's what the black man's name tag read—took hold of my father's wrist and motioned with his head for me to leave.

I turned away from my father's cries to help him, turned my back and ran out the same blue door, punching my way through. I took a deep breath then retched beside my bike.

I leaned my bike against the garage wall and stepped into my backyard. My sister had come home; she stood behind my mother, delicately braiding her graying hair. I could see the bandage on her hand.

"*Mãe*, he wants to come home. We need to bring him home."

There was no response. It was cold but I took off my windbreaker and threw off my sweatshirt. I sat on the flagstone walkway that connected the house to the garage and then to the laneway. I kicked off my shoes and flung off my socks. I lay back flat on the path with my arms to my sides and looked up into the dotted sky. Its beauty was in its vastness, places unseen, distances unchallenged.

Their faces, too, were turned up into the starlit sky. A cool wind began to blow. There was whimsy in their eyes. My mother's large whirligig rattled atop the flagpole. The girl with the bangs in the painted dress spun in a cartwheel, arms and legs splayed open. Behind her was a figure that looked like Jesus without a beard, dressed all in white with red stains on its hands and robe. The fisherman reeled in his line of fish—the many small fish that he held on his line—before dropping it once again over the side of his small boat named *Avé*. The boy sat on his bike and pedaled with determination, a need to go somewhere, anywhere. Together, the propellers twirled while the figures worked in their fruitless pantomime.

~ MR. WONG PRESENTS JESUS ~

MY FATHER BEAMED AS HE held the tickets in the shape of a fan—*pick-a-card, any-card.* He laid them on the kitchen table with a rap of his knuckles. CN RAIL— Economy: Toronto to Niagara Falls. I had never ridden on a train. The last time we were all together on any kind of trip was when we went to Portugal to bury my grandmother. I was six then and my memories were nothing more than broken scenes: being bathed in half-barrels of cold water, soft butter, dirty feet, long worn faces, heat and sweat and dust, bread torn by hand, animals and blood, laundry soap, outhouses with neat piles of assorted rags, hockey-stick sideburns, Aunt Candy—her red lips framing crooked teeth, my grandmother like a lump of charcoal—cursed and blamed with every small gasp.

"It's certainly not B.C.," I said. I raised my eyes and continued to cross-hatch my sketch. My father rolled up his sleeves and scoured his hands under hot water like a surgeon. A trip to Niagara Falls on Christmas Eve wasn't exactly the train ride he had been promising all our lives: sweeping across Canada, west to the Rockies. He came back and stood between my mother and me, clean-shaven, looking out the window at an already darkening sky. His white shirt so crisp and fresh. He reminded me of the early black-and-white pictures he had of himself, posing outside Toronto's city hall in a tailored suit and dark overcoat and fedora. That big smile of his that puffed out his cheeks. Or with his plaid shirts and pleated trousers in the middle of Canada's wilderness, his foot on top of a bear he had shot dead near the rails in Kenora. Or so he said.

"What are you drawing?" he asked.

I continued to dig my pencil into the paper, short quick strokes. "It's a bird—a dead one."

I had found it last week, crumpled against the curb at the foot of Bathurst where I liked to go every so often on my bike to draw or read. I had found a bag in the garbage and brought it home. It was still in the box freezer in the basement, frozen with its broken wing tipped upward and its head tucked under its breast.

"I no see a bird. I see crazy lines but I no see a bird."

"You wouldn't," I said.

"Why you no do math? I no come to this country for you to make pictures of birds."

My ears were burning. He knew I wanted to draw. Even though my teachers told him I was special, had a real gift, he always snorted his anger in the same way. "Business," he'd say, "he will be a businessman."

I spent most of my time in my room with the radio cranked, a bulging capsule of bass.

My mother sat beside him, not close, but near enough that she could reach to brush his leg. He lowered his head and she whispered something.

"Very nice, *filho*," he said, straightening himself.

He hadn't had a drink in over a year now, had found work as a custodian at the Eaton Centre.

"Too late," I said. I scooped up my charcoal and pencils, flipped my sketch pad shut, and pushed my chair away from the table.

"He wants this for us, and he's been so good," she had said when my sister had blurted, "I won't go." My sister was twenty and saw herself as a woman who couldn't be led any longer; she would make decisions for herself. But a private conversation with my mother had made her pack her bag and she sat slumped next to me trying to read a trashy novel.

Every time a relative of ours came to Canada, Niagara Falls was the first place we'd take them. My father got a kick out of hearing their "oohs" and their "ahhh, *mas que maravilha.*" And I knew he measured the success of the trip by the number of camera clicks as they posed holding on to the leaves of a branch, knee-highs flattening the hair on their legs or men in shiny suits on a hot day. My father took great pride in possessing the photographic precision needed to create the illusion of holding the Skyline Tower in their hands like the Statue of Liberty.

They would all come from Portugal smelling of salt and damp cotton, like the end of my sleeve I would catch myself sucking when I was a kid. They lived with us for the first little while; "just until they get their feet on the ground" was what my mother used to say, without the slightest trace of her sticky Portuguese accent. They all stayed rent-free for a couple of months, but never much more than that; there was always another letter informing my father his sponsorship had been approved by Canadian immigration officials, announcing that another family member was waiting with fresh passport in hand.

It became a lonely place when our big house on Palmerston Avenue remained empty. Rooms were cleaned with water and bleach, sheets were changed, before everything was covered with plastic or drop cloths and the doors were shut and locked, sealed like a vacuum, waiting for the next relative.

All that had stopped when I was about ten. Now that they were here, the relatives hardly visited. My father had said some awful things to them, hurtful things. For the most part we were alone and had only each other.

During the train ride, few words were exchanged. My mother smiled and squeezed my father's arm every time he looked her way. Our sullen expressions and sighs of boredom went ignored. My father excused himself and announced he needed to go to the bathroom. He walked down the aisle, steadying himself on the backs of the seats.

"You need to know something. Your father came to this country with nothing—knowing no one. He came with a dream. He made a good life for himself, for your sister and you and me. Your father is a proud man; he's proud of us all."

I didn't want to start anything.

"I know your father loves you. But life, *a vida,* was not supposed to be this way for him. Your father made big dreams for himself in Canada. The ones he helped come to this country are now doing much better than him; their dreams have come true. It's not easy for him. Try to understand."

"So what was his dream?" I asked.

"I'm not sure anymore, *filho.*"

When we arrived my father struggled to read the signs at the train station, and I could tell he resigned himself to moving with the flow of the other passengers on our train. He hailed a cab from the platform. He did it with such flair, as if it was the kind of thing he was accustomed to. His regained confidence put me at ease in a strange way. He simply said, "To the Falls, please."

My father opened the cab door for my mother. I could hear the deep roaring of the great Falls. The mist had frozen on the trees that lined the river's edge. They looked like glass cages, crystallized branches that reached down to touch the snow. The Falls were lit, a mass of color blocks—red, blue, pink, green—that seemed to pulse underneath the raging water that tumbled over the brink. What looked like an iceberg shaped in a semicircle had formed above the cataract that deflected huge amounts of water into the gorge, a stunning backdrop of white thundered down below. Even my sister leaned over the gorge's railing and grinned, her breath streaming from between her teeth.

I remembered a story from a school trip; an Indian woman had stepped into her canoe and, singing her death song softly to herself, paddled into the current and hurtled toward the Falls. But the gods or something like that saved her, and the rainbow became her gift to the people. *It's the kind of shit you just can't make up,* I thought.

The Chinese lanterns hung in perfect rows over the tables, their red fringe swaying to our footsteps as we were led to a booth. It was clear the restaurant had once been a kind of fifties diner; some of the old touches were still there: quilted stainless steel in the kitchen peek-through, jukeboxes in the booths—ours was stuck on a Patsy Cline page: "Sweet Dreams," "I Fall to Pieces," and "Just a Closer Walk with Thee"—the Rolodex handles that flipped the pages long broken. The owners had tried to infuse the place with Chinese touches: scrolls of slashed writing, large plastic flower arrangements, the plucky music that played in the background, and the orange glow of paper lanterns across the red wallpaper and vinyl booths. The owners had made it into something they wanted, reinvented the place and breathed life into it.

The restaurant was empty, except for an old man who sat near the front. It was freezing outside and he looked out the window running with condensation. He slurped his twisted noodles as if eating spaghetti. He had no teeth and I couldn't look because the way he ate with his gums reminded me of other old people, of my Grandmother

Theresa who had died only two months earlier and for
whom my mother still wore black, and would most likely
continue to do for the full two years she was obligated. It
was the only place open that late on Christmas Eve, Mr.
Wong's.

My sister shimmied along the vinyl bench patched with
squares of duct tape. She bumped me over and smiled.

"Where did your father go?" my mother asked.

"He's by the phone, *Mãe*," I replied at the same time
my sister said, "Looking for a liquor store that's open."

My mother scowled at her. "Your father hasn't had a
drink in a year." Her quick retort clearly indicated how
anxious she was, uncertain of how the holiday would play
itself out. "It's important that he know we appreciate how
much he wanted to do this for us."

My sister flipped through the menu.

"I'm going to the bathroom," I said.

I stopped by a large aquarium. Three carp barely
moved within its velvety green walls. They looked bored.
Beside it was a nativity scene, lit with Christmas lights
that sliced through the cracks in the crèche walls and lay
in colorful lines across the gathered figures. They looked
like they were at a disco. They were made of blue and
white porcelain and they all looked Chinese, with their
thinly painted eyes. I couldn't help but smile.

"The greatest gift," someone whispered. I almost
expected him to finish off with *Little Grasshopper*. I looked
back and saw it was Mr. Wong—I assumed that was his
name—the man who had earlier shown us to our booth
and handed us our menus. His hair was cut too short; it
stuck out at the back. He wore gold-rimmed spectacles

that made me want to trust him. His yellow fingers reached in and lifted the Chinese Jesus. He reached for my hand, uncurled my fingers, and placed the tiny figurine in my palm. I motioned that I couldn't but he closed my fingers over its smoothness and wouldn't accept my refusal.

"A gift of life. The cycle of birth and death. He is a great symbol of sacrifice." He closed his eyes and it was as if he was praying or casting some kind of mental blessing, holding my hand tight as he did.

Embarrassed, I slid Jesus into my pocket. My father half-grinned as he saw me approach, rolled his shoulder away from me and lowered his voice on the pay phone. I made my way into the bathroom. The shocking white and fluorescent lights popped me into a new reality. The bathroom walls were littered with old newspapers that had been glued, I thought, but on closer inspection I realized it was wallpaper made to look like a collage of old newspapers. The stories were all about the same thing: Niagara Falls stunts and daredevils, with graphic sepia-toned photographs of men crossing the Falls on a tightrope, holding a long pole for balance, or various concoctions of boats and barrels and the happy faces of the heroes, the ones who had made it over safely. There were other, more gruesome photographs of the many who had died trying, curled up in crumpled balls within their barrel walls or puffed and bloated after being dredged up weeks later. I was fascinated. It was then that my ears adjusted to my father's muffled questions and curses coming through the paper-thin doors.

"Nothing? Not one room for four peoples—impossible—nothing at all? . . . Train station closed—where I go? Where my family going to go? . . . I want to speak to manager. Hello . . . hello." He crashed the receiver into its holder just as I walked by shaking my wet hands in the air.

"Why you no dry your hands in the washroom?"

"Didn't you reserve a hotel?"

He grabbed the side of my head. At sixteen I was now taller than him. He drew my face close to his.

"I make everything okay. You hear me?" It was a threat that had been spurred by my challenge: stupidity, incompetence, failure, whatever judgment it was that he had registered in my voice.

"Let go!" I said.

"Why can't those canaries shut up?" Terri moved her hands to her temples. "It's like a fucken zoo in here."

"Watch you mouth. You is nineteen but that no mean you—"

"I'm twenty."

My father looked wounded, but only for a moment.

"Manuel." My mother playfully flicked at his cufflink. "What should we eat? I don't know anything . . ."

My father turned to stare out the window.

"Can I take your order?" Mr. Wong bowed.

"I'd like the chicken balls with—"

"Terezinha, your father will make the order for our food," my mother said.

My sister dropped the menu and made small circles with her fingertips at her temples.

"Mr. Wong?" I felt stupid the minute I spoke the words. "Is there some way we can stop the noise from the birds? My sister here—"

"Oh, this not noise," Mr. Wong said.

"Squawking, chirping, whatever. Could you just get them to stop?" Terri piped up.

"Sometimes beautiful song cover up deep hurt," Mr. Wong said.

Terri chuckled. "Confucius say . . ." she added.

I thought my father was going to jump out of his seat and strangle her.

"Birds in cages sing. To some, sound like beautiful song. But we do not know; we do not have the words," Mr. Wong added. "A great puzzle."

"These Chinese, they is smart people." I could see my father tapping his forehead through the veil from the steaming noodles. "They come to this country with nothing and live like animals, twenty, maybe thirty in one house. Like dogs they work, in restaurants or factories, whatever, and no complaints. They is cheap and they save everything they can. Before you know they no wear their short pants and Chinese slippers anymore. No. They buy leather shoes and expensive gabardines. They pay for houses in cash-money. They is smart these people, I tell you."

My mother had managed to eat a couple of shrimp but refused to touch the noodles my father had ordered.

"I can't, Manuel, I'm full," my mother said as she continued to draw the noodles to the edge of her plate. I knew she thought they looked like cats' guts. She used to say that Chinese people ate cats, and whenever a cat went missing, there was always a well-fed family somewhere in our neighborhood.

"*Mãe*, these are noodles," I offered.

"Leave your mother. If she want to eat, she eat," my father said.

"This is nice," my mother said.

"Oh, this is nothing. When I traveled across Canada on a train, so beautiful this country. You no see nothing like this in the world. It take the breath out of me."

"Not completely," Terri mumbled.

"Is that it? My children laugh at me?"

"No, Manuel, they just—"

"I know what they is doing."

The silence was broken by his fist hitting the table. "You no know how much I had in me. You can't see." His voice shook. "I leave Portugal on fishing boat and I know I not going to come back. I give everything away to follow something new. I no understand what but something inside push me here—to make something of myself in this land. I come to be someone in this world. *If you are going to* fazer uma América *then let this country shape you.* That is what Mateus say to me one day."

"Who's that?" I asked.

My father looked at my mother. "I almost lose my life once when I come to this country. I push off from the *Argus* into the ocean. Three days," he roared, "I float in the open waters until a storm come and rip into me and my boat and I let go . . . dropped to the bottom of the sea . . ."

I wasn't quite sure if he paused for dramatic effect or if the recollection was overwhelming him. It didn't matter; I just wanted the elusive story that I had heard only in snippets throughout my life.

"But I is saved. I turn my back on everything I know to make a life in Canada. Do you understand how hard that is for me?"

"*Pai*." I surprised myself by referring to him in Portuguese. "There are people that have gone over the Falls in a barrel and they've survived."

As if on cue my mother made the sign of the cross and piped up, "Never. Those are crazy people."

He wavered, looked at my sister sternly, uncertain if he should be drawn in by my deflection. "Not exactly." My father had taken the bait. "Is true there is adventure in all of us." My mother looked unconvinced. "Everyone has adventure in the brains and in the heart and it make some men famous, rich even."

"Don't forget dead," my sister added, wiping the corners of her mouth.

"*Mãe*, they go over in a barrel and the barrel is filled with padding and pillows so I think you just come out of—"

"Balance, *filho*. No forget balance. This is most important. I say you have to know how the barrel goes over, in what direction and angle." My father seemed pleased with the turn in discussion.

"I think it's stupid," my mother said. "You can die."

My father looked incredulous. I knew she was playing along with it. But his tone was becoming insulting, and soon even she wouldn't want to play any longer.

"A man need to make a mark in this world. You still no understand," he said. "Women no understand these things. A man have dreams." He stared at the water-stained ceiling and scratched his stubbly neck with his knuckles.

Mr. Wong came over to clear the table. He left four fortune cookies on a small dish and took the thirty dollars my father had laid on the table. He was leaving Mr. Wong a seventy-eight-cent tip and waved him off as if he should be pleased with his generosity.

"*A closed mouth gathers no feet,*" my sister read. She crumpled the fortune between her fingers then flicked it across the table. "What the hell does that mean?"

My mother copied the way we had cracked our cookies, then handed the paper to me to read. *A dream is not responsible to the one who believes in it.* My mother crunched on the cookie and looked pleased.

"Let me see mine. *Thing are lost when not used.*"

"Ooooh, like your manhood," my sister smirked.

"Shut up!"

"Why you no be more of lady, like your mother. I no want to remember Christmas like this." My father's strong hand had pinned my sister's hand to the table.

"Manuel, Manuel, Manuel," my mother whispered through clenched teeth as she scanned the room to see if anyone was looking.

"There is no one here, *Mãe,*" I said.

"You no have respect! You make fun of everything I say." He pressed down hard, his arm rigid.

I grabbed him by the wrist. "Let go," I said as I squeezed harder and wedged his hand open. He drew his trembling hand away then tucked it under the table. My sister glared at him. She was not afraid.

"Who make sure there is food on the table?" he began. "Who give you school, to teach you right and wrong, huh?"

My mother started moving in her seat, rolled from one ass cheek to the other.

"Manuel, everyone is tired," she pleaded.

"I no come to this country to make a life for myself and for you to laugh and throw this in my face like paper you clean your ass with." His voice was raised. Mr. Wong and the cook remained in the kitchen area.

"You is good-for-nothing—all of you. After all the things I do for you. A nice house, clothes, and—"

I blurted a laugh, a quick snort that made his head snap in my direction. It stunned my mother and sister both. But for once there was no reprimand, and there was no use backpedaling.

"You think it was easy for us. All you talk about is how hard it was and *when you were my age* and all that martyr shit. But did you ever think how hard it was for me? How hard it still is to try and live a dream you never claimed?"

"*Filho!*" my mother interjected softly.

I raised a hand to stop her. My father sat silent; his face betrayed nothing and, in so doing, welcomed me to push further. I leaned over the table, moved closer to him until I could clearly see the spider-like veins that crept across his nose and cheeks.

"Do you even know what I want out of life? Does it even matter?"

He looked straight at me. I could hear the blood pulsing in my ears. The room began to spin, brilliant lights that wobbled in my head. The only figure that stood clear and resolute was that of my father. His silence was beginning to drain the power I thought I held over him. I was uncertain of what I had done.

"I'm tired," my sister yawned. "Let's check in to the hotel."

"More like the train station," I said.

My father's scowl moved over me. He was disgusted with my betrayal. It was the same expression I had gazed upon all my life. He didn't want to understand. The love was there, but only beneath the bruised surface of our relationship.

"Manuel?"

"That's great! That's just fucken remarkable." My father did not flinch at my sister's outburst, her choice of words. "Stranded here in Niagara Falls on the coldest day of the year and nowhere to go." Terri began to scramble through her purse, pushing the contents aside, looking for something.

"Manuel, we'll have to go home," my mother said.

I buried my face in my hands, scratched my itchy scalp with my palms. I was tired and just wanted to disappear, wanted them all to just disappear.

"I'm calling Luis. He'll pick us up."

Luis was my sister's boyfriend. She had been invited to spend Christmas Eve with his family this year, had accepted then had been embarrassed to have to say no.

She moved to the pay phone. On her way she grabbed a folded tablecloth, snapped it into the air, and draped the suspended canary cage with it. "Driving me fucken nuts."

"*One cannot lose something they never had,*" my father whispered, then flicked his fortune on the table. He had rubbed the narrow strip of paper between his thumb and forefinger until it coiled like a tiny spring. It sat on the table slowly unraveling. The snow had begun to fall. It was dark now.

"*Pai*, I didn't mean—"

"I know, *filho*, I know," he replied, his eyes fixed on the window, brimming with tears. "This not the place for old mans, is for the young and strong."

"As long as we're together. That's the most important thing." My mother wove her arm with my father's. He did not resist.

"Only a few people have ever survived the Falls."

I waited but there was no answer.

"I read on the bathroom walls about the stunts that happened over the Falls," I continued, but still there was only this ominous silence. "They became famous. But how could you survive?" I was trying to tangle myself in his web so he could show me his superior knowledge of science or brilliance in engineering. He liked nothing more. I thought it would knock my father out of his strange daze, alleviate the concern carved on my mother's forehead.

"*Pai*, did you hear me?"

He looked at us and smiled generously.

"I can't get a hold of him. They've probably gone to midnight mass," Terri said.

"Oh my, it's time. Manuel, I saw a church before we came, St. Elizabeth's, I think."

My father nodded.

He stood up, reached for his wool coat and buttoned it with one hand. We were all shuffling out of the booth, still caught somewhat off guard by his quiet but agreeable nature. We heard the door swing open; curled wisps of snow streamed in as he left.

The three of us huddled and walked headfirst into the blustering wind. The icy snow pelted our faces. I raised a forearm across my brow and caught the almost ghostly figure of my father walking against the storm. He turned left from Victoria Street onto Clifton Hill, walked in the direction of all the old horror shops and souvenir places that sold pencil sharpeners in the shape of the Maid of the Mist and little Indian dolls with fur-trimmed parkas rimming dark-skinned faces. He would disappear for a moment, then his silhouette would take shape once again through another blast of wind and snow that dragged its nets down the empty road, trawling for scattered garbage: coffee cups, newspapers, leaflets, lost gloves.

We had dressed for the cold but not for the snow. My mother had wanted to look nice for the weekend. She had worn her black suede heels that she kept in a velour bag with a drawstring and only wore to funerals. She almost tiptoed along the sidewalk, careful of where her feet came down.

The road descended toward the lip of the gorge and its lookout points with stand-up binoculars, twenty-five cents for five minutes. I could see my father leaning against the thick railing.

"The church is not here, Manuel," my mother said. But a gust of wind hit her open mouth, forced her to swallow the frigid air. She turned from him, shielded herself as she pleaded, "My toes, Manuel. They're frozen."

"This is better than the church," he said as he smiled. He swept his arm over the railing as if slowly casting grass seed. "So beautiful."

It was a magical sight; the thunderous roar of the Falls, the mist that crystallized wherever it settled, and the snow, huge snowflakes that now spun and twisted in a gentler wind. It was Christmas Eve and I thought of what the evening had meant two thousand years ago, how everything must have been heightened for Mary and Joseph on the eve of that birth; how, denied a place to stay for the night, the miracle was born.

When I turned from the railing, my father had moved on, dragging his hand along the thick iron that stood between the tourists and the Falls. He turned to look at us. My sister was a bit farther behind, crouched with my mother, arm in arm, making slow headway against the wind.

I could hear my father singing something, a fado from long ago about life and love and things lost and all that other crap my family spoke of incessantly. He was walking with purpose, confidently placing one foot in front of the other, certain of where he was heading. We were close to the park by the river where we would often picnic with our family, near the botanical gardens where the women would go with their scraps of tinfoil looking for seeds or samples to pinch and bring home.

My father stood by a large tree, held his arm high on its thick trunk and leaned against it. I was out of breath when I got to him, only to find soft billowing puffs, slow and controlled, coming from his nostrils. He looked out across the river, to the American side. My mother and sister caught up to us finally.

"Manuel," my mother panted, "it's cold. We need to go."

"Is this why we came, to look at a river in the dead of winter? Is this the trip you've wanted to give us all your life?" My sister laid into him. She was oblivious to my mother's tug on her coat.

My father turned and looked at us. His face appeared raw, and the snowflakes fell on his cheeks and lashes and melted. His mouth widened and his teeth broke through his parted lips.

As he hummed, his legs began to move as though he were going to do our traditional folkdance of two-stepping and twirls followed by clapping over the shoulder. He slid his fingers into his coat and unbuttoned it in what seemed like a swoop, dropped it over his shoulders onto the film of snow at his feet.

"Manuel?" my mother whispered.

He used his toes to wedge the heels of his shoes and took them off. He slipped off his socks and rolled them into little balls, tucked one in each shoe. The white tops of his feet melded with the snow.

He turned and walked to the shore.

"Manuel! Are you crazy? Manuel! . . . Antonio, go get him, *filho*," my mother cried.

But I could not move, remained fixed like the thick trunks that surrounded me. The wind whipped a stray grocery bag and old newspaper against the masts of maples and oaks.

My sister picked up my father's shoes, rubbed their supple tongues, and draped his coat over her shoulder. My mother took two steps, reached forward at the

same time my father walked onto the ice that rimmed
the shore. He looked back. His forehead glowed under
the moon's light. *I love him for the man that he can be*, I
thought.

My hand darted out of my pocket. I lifted my arm
into the air to wave, caught myself holding Mr. Wong's
baby Jesus, all swaddled in lint.

My father turned away.

"Every song has a fire in it," he sang. *"A fiery dream that
burns."*

Acknowledgments

The following works have been invaluable to me: *I Sailed with Portugal's Captain Courageous* (National Geographic, 1952); *The Lonely Doryman* (National Geographic, 1968); Carlos Teixeira and Victor M. P. Da Rosa, ed., *The Portuguese in Canada: From the Sea to the City* (University of Toronto Press, 2000). I would also like to acknowledge the passionate words and voices of fado singers that keep the tradition alive: Dulce Pontes, Christina Branco, Mariza, Cesaria Evora, and Amalia Rodrigues—it is for you that fado is written.

Although this book is a work of fiction, inspired by research, relationships and family histories, I have taken liberties with places and people depicted in this book to frame a story. Also, I have simplified the reproduction of a particular Portuguese dialect that was part of *my* childhood—of my world. If there are any inaccuracies, they are my own.

To the many people who were instrumental at the start of my writing journey, including Ania Szado, Brad Reed, and Cynthia Holtz. To other writers who provided valuable feedback and encouragement and who helped shape these fledgling stories. Thank you. I would like to acknowledge the editors at the following publications in which portions of this book first appeared: the *Dalhousie Review, Descant, Paperplates,* and the *Nashwaak Review.*

Thanks to David Whiteside, who quietly takes care of everything, and to Emily Shorthouse, who read *Shoeshine Boy* as an intern at Descant and introduced me to my literary agent, Denise Bukowski, always a tireless guardian of my work—I appreciate everything you do.

To everyone at Doubleday Canada who has been so generous and supportive, including Martha Leonard, Susan Broadhurst, Terri Nimmo, Kristin Cochrane, Susan Burns, and Nicola Makoway. I'd like to thank Maya Mavjee for her resolute confidence, and especially Martha Kanya-Forstner for her editorial insight, passion and guidance. I am deeply indebted. I'd also like to thank Jane Rosenman, my American editor, for believing in this story and for championing *Barnacle Love.*

I would like to thank my sister for our shared childhood and for her understanding, and my family for their strength and courage in a new land.

Finally, I could not have written this book without the help of my wife, Stephanie. Her love and belief in the stories I wanted to tell inspired me. And to my three sons, Julian, Oliver and Simon, who show me every day that I am loved and blessed.

BARNACLE LOVE

The Burden:
A Note from the Author

Questions for Discussion

~ *THE BURDEN* ~

A Note from the Author

In 1988 my mother and I traveled to São Miguel, Azores. I had been a boy when we last visited twenty years before. I was twenty-two now. My father had passed away a couple of years earlier. My mother had hoped to return to the Azores to divest herself and our family of land and property that tied us to an unrecognizable homeland. Only then could she fully realize a life for herself in Canada. But it was there, through the winding, dusty roads that snaked their way toward my parents' village of Lomba da Maia that I discovered being Portuguese *was in me*—something that could not be forced or taught, and could not be so easily severed. I had never felt the connection before. Much of my identity was determined by my parents, who my grandparents were, and the soil that nurtured them.

Growing up in Toronto with Portuguese parents was defined by living in secret and separate worlds. Most of the clashes, certainly all of my internal conflict, arose from an inability to bridge the great divide between the ethnic culture I inherited and the Canadian culture I felt was my birthright. I lived in two distinct cultural contexts: my Portuguese heritage shrouded behind our front door and my Canadian identity, which I felt most comfortable in the minute I closed our front gate behind me.

As our taxi drove into the village, a plume of swirling dust in our wake, relatives and villagers lined the small road leading to my ancestral home. In their faces I could not help but see those early Portuguese immigrants. My father emigrated to provide a better future for himself and eventually his wife, children, and even parents and siblings. Leaving a family behind must have been difficult, a decision that carried a burden of guilt. For my father, the voyage did not devastate his identity like it had for so many others. He refused to become a stranger to himself and chose to embrace his new life in Canada. And as I got out of the taxi to greet a family I did not know, I was struck by their generosity and welcoming spirit. It was at that moment that I could not help but think that my father must have been haunted by some sense of loss, that his choice had in effect barred him from claiming his past, a world that no longer existed for him.

I'm certain he felt confusion and anxiety—the result of being marginalized and alienated. Alone, he was forced to assimilate into English Canada. There was no choice for these early pioneers. He worked on Canada's national railway and found himself drifting across a vast land with little connection to the place and people he left behind. Although my father often looked back on those days as times of hard work, I believe his wistful reminisces were his attempts at reclaiming the shattered images of what he had left, what he had lost, and what he wanted to reinvent for himself. He lived in an in-between world. Who was he? How could he identify himself?

We entered a small, whitewashed house that day, located at the end of a road and perched above a cliff that looks out onto an expanse of blue. We stood around a small table in a stifling kitchen, were greeted with hearty hugs and tears. My mother stood out in her floral dress and heels. There was discomfort in her face—an uncertainty in her step. My mother had straddled both worlds: the Old World, with its traditions and customs, and her new world in Canada, which she had forged through marriage with my father. At times, my mother had voiced regret for not achieving "more," for not seizing the opportunity to go to school in Canada. Like many immigrant parents, my mother was forced to live a necessary illusion. Her life in Canada was defined by a marriage to a man she barely knew. She had simply become my father's link to a place he had allowed to slip from his fingers. She coped by focusing her energies on her children and "suffered secretly." Sadly, it became *our* reluctant inheritance—to carry out unfulfilled dreams as the first generation of immigrants grieved their lost hopes, dashed dreams.

Barnacle Love is an exploration of both the intended promise and the disappointment inherent in the choices made by a father and the expectations he places on his son. Manuel is any immigrant, every immigrant, always reaching for a dream he cannot have. Intimate and personal, the story of the Rebelo family is the story of the forces that tear many immigrant families apart. At its heart is a story of a boy unwilling to carry the burden of his father's unfulfilled dreams.

~ *QUESTIONS FOR DISCUSSION* ~

1. How does the author's writing demonstrate what Manuel is going through, what the world looks and feels like to him? How does the tone and style in the first half, "Terra Nova," differ from that in the section that follows, "Caged Birds Sing"? Discuss how the switch in narrative voice heightens the reader's understanding of the central themes.

2. "The Portuguese call it *saudade:* a longing for something so indefinite as to be indefinable. Love affairs, miseries of life, the way things were, people already dead, those who left and the ocean that tossed them on the shores of a different land—all things born of the soul that can only be felt" (page 4). What past feelings, experiences, places, or events now trigger Manuel's senses

and make him remember? Is the indescribable feeling of *saudade* evident in any other characters? Is this something you have experienced in your own life?

3. How much responsibility do you think Manuel's mother, Maria Theresa da Conceição Rebelo, bears for what happens to her son? How much of his behavior is genetically driven, and how much results from his mother's influence and the circumstances of his upbringing? How does Manuel's abuse at the hands of a priest contribute to the person he becomes?

4. What is the significance of the title *Barnacle Love*? In what ways are each of the central characters bound to tradition? Discuss the difficulties encountered by immigrants trying to preserve their Old World ways in their new land.

5. Manuel begins his journey with such hope and promise for a new life. The reader is drawn to this man who is filled with the dream of making it in America. What happens to his dream?

6. "Caged Birds Sing" invites readers into the lives of the Rebelos and finds there both the promise and the disappointment inherent in the choices made by the father and the expectations placed on his son. How does this section develop the theme of freedom?

7. In literature, it is the intimate unwritten world of a character that is often more intriguing than the words on the page. There is a span of time—almost ten years—between Manuel's life in Newfoundland and his return with his family to the Azores to bear witness to his mother's death. What has happened during this time? As readers, can we fill in the gaps in the lives of these characters? Is it even important to know, or is it fair for the author to burden the reader with creating histories based on the reader's experiences?

8. The roles of men and women are sharply drawn in *Barnacle Love*. Discuss what the role of gender is in the novel and how identity is shaped, not only by gender, but also by the settings: the isolated Azores in the middle of the Atlantic, Newfoundland, and a modern city like Toronto. Discuss the ways in which the settings function as characters in the novel and how each of the characters relate to those settings.

9. Colm Tóibín wrote, "Anthony De Sa moves with skill and ingenuity between folk tale, myth, and narratives of contemporary displacement. The tone is spare and elegiac; the stories are filled with carefully chosen details and sharply drawn characters. They have immense emotional and powerful truths." Discuss how the author reveals the theme of displacement through the powerful truths of Manuel, Georgina, Terezinha, and Antonio.

10. In "Mr. Wong Presents Jesus" Antonio asks his mother "So what was his dream?" and she responds "I'm not sure anymore, *filho*" (page 199). The novel ends with Manuel singing *"Every song has a fire in it . . . a fiery dream that burns"* (page 214). The reader is left to contemplate their "dreams." Is this true for all of us? Do we all dream? Do we ever really know what it is we long for? Discuss your fiery dream.

GEORGE PIMENTEL

Anthony De Sa grew up in Toronto's Portuguese community. *Barnacle Love* was a finalist for both the 2008 Scotiabank Giller Prize and the 2009 Toronto Book Award. He lives in Toronto with his wife and their three sons.

Other Algonquin Readers Round Table Novels

A Reliable Wife, a novel by Robert Goolrick

Rural Wisconsin, 1907. In the bitter cold, Ralph Truitt stands alone on a train platform anxiously awaiting the arrival of the woman who answered his newspaper ad for "a reliable wife." The woman who arrives is not the one he expects in this *New York Times* #1 Bestseller about love and madness, longing and murder.

"[A] chillingly engrossing plot . . . Good to the riveting end."
—*USA Today*

"Deliciously wicked and tense . . . Intoxicating." —*The Washington Post*

"A rousing historical potboiler." —*The Boston Globe*

AN ALGONQUIN READERS ROUND TABLE EDITION WITH READING GROUP GUIDE AND OTHER SPECIAL FEATURES • FICTION • ISBN 978-1-56512-977-1

Between Here and April, a novel by Deborah Copaken Kogan

When a deep-rooted memory suddenly surfaces, Elizabeth Burns becomes obsessed with the long-ago disappearance of her childhood friend April Cassidy.

"The perfect book club book." —*The Washington Post Book World*

"[A] haunting page-turner . . . [A] compelling look at what it means to be a mother and a wife." —*Working Mother*

"Extraordinary . . . This is a story that needs to be told."
—*Elle,* #1 Reader's Pick

AN ALGONQUIN READERS ROUND TABLE EDITION WITH READING GROUP GUIDE AND OTHER SPECIAL FEATURES • FICTION • ISBN 978-1-56512-932-0

Every Last Cuckoo, a novel by Kate Maloy

In the tradition of Jane Smiley and Sue Miller comes this wise and gratifying novel about a woman who gracefully accepts a surprising new role in life just when she thinks her best years are behind her.

Winner of the ALA Reading List Award for Women's Fiction

"Truly engrossing . . . an excellent book club selection." —*Library Journal*

"A tender and wise story of what happens when love lasts."
—Katharine Weber, author of *Triangle*

"Inspiring . . . Grabs the reader by the heart."
—*The New Orleans Times-Picayune*

AN ALGONQUIN READERS ROUND TABLE EDITION WITH READING GROUP GUIDE AND OTHER SPECIAL FEATURES • FICTION • ISBN 978-1-56512-675-6

Mudbound, a novel by Hillary Jordan

Mudbound is the saga of the McAllen family, who struggle to survive on a remote ramshackle farm, and the Jacksons, their black sharecroppers. When two sons return from World War II to work the land, the unlikely friendship between these brothers-in-arms—one white, one black—arouses the passions of their neighbors. In this award-winning portrait of two families caught up in the blind hatred of a small Southern town, prejudice takes many forms, both subtle and ruthless.

Winner of the Bellwether Prize for Fiction

"This is storytelling at the height of its powers . . . Hillary Jordan writes with the force of a Delta storm." —Barbara Kingsolver

AN ALGONQUIN READERS ROUND TABLE EDITION WITH READING GROUP GUIDE AND OTHER SPECIAL FEATURES • FICTION • ISBN 978-1-56512-677-0

Water for Elephants, a novel by Sara Gruen

As a young man, Jacob Jankowski is tossed by fate onto a rickety train, home to the Benzini Brothers Most Spectacular Show on Earth. Amid a world of freaks, grifters, and misfits, Jacob becomes involved with Marlena, the beautiful young equestrian star; her husband, a charismatic but twisted animal trainer; and Rosie, an untrainable elephant who is the great gray hope for this third-rate show. Now in his nineties, Jacob at long last reveals the story of their unlikely yet powerful bond, one that nearly shatters them all.

"[An] arresting new novel . . .With a showman's expert timing, [Gruen] saves a terrific revelation for the final pages, transforming a glimpse of Americana into an enchanting escapist fairy tale."
—*The New York Times Book Review*

AN ALGONQUIN READERS ROUND TABLE EDITION WITH READING GROUP GUIDE AND OTHER SPECIAL FEATURES • FICTION • ISBN 978-1-56512-560-5